By Palmer Jc

A Southern Kind of Love Series:

O'Keeley's Irish Pub Series:

HER IRISH BOSS

O'KEELEY'S IRISH PUB: BOOK ONE

PALMER JONES

SWEET BLOOMS PUBLISHING, LLC

Print Edition: 978-1-7333968-1-3

E-Book Edition: 978-1-7333968-0-6

Cover design by JD&J Design.

Editing by Patricia Ogilvie.

First Edition

For M&A

1

"**U**nreasonable, heartless bastard."

Those were the last words Brogan O'Keeley heard as the cook he fired shoved open the front door and tossed his apron on the ground. The waitress scurried along behind him, her head held high; she was quiet. She hadn't said much after Brogan walked in on them in the supply closet, undressed down to their knickers. Some things he wished he could unsee. Even though he was Irish, he didn't approve of men's boxers dotted with shamrocks.

Brogan glanced around his restaurant, making eye contact with any employee who still stood in shock, watching the unnecessary drama instead of ensuring O'Keeley's Irish Pub was ready to receive customers.

As he buttoned his suit jacket, Brogan noted it was one minute until they opened for lunch. It'd been a hell of a morning already, but working, driving forward in life, always centered him. Staying in control. Managing day-to-day operations. He was good at both of those.

The man said he was unreasonable. Probably. The good of his company would always override rule-breakers who put his business at risk, possibly leaving them open to a sexual harassment lawsuit.

And if anyone asked his brothers, they'd both agree that he was a heartless bastard. He'd devoted the past ten years to make this restaurant a success. For himself. For his brothers. He worked hard to make sure O'Keeley's Irish Pub was ready to present the best possible experience to its customers. Perfection was achievable—

"Sorry!"

Brogan closed his eyes. And timeliness was everything.

But not to Selena. He took a breath to ensure his voice was even. Too much of his accent and it might give away his irritation.

"I got here—"

"As soon as you could," he finished for her. He opened his eyes, hoping to see Selena at least ready to wait on customers. Nope. Too much to ask. Her white shirt with the O'Keely's Irish Pub logo was untucked. She held her sneakers in her hands, bright pink flip flops peeking out from underneath her blue jeans.

Her hair, a honey color, long and loose around her shoulders, was not pulled back and meeting safety guidelines. The snap of attraction each day he set eyes on her still irritated him. He clenched his teeth. Personal feelings were always separate from conducting business. He'd paid too much the last time he blurred the lines.

She grimaced. "Yes. I'm really sorry, Mr. O'Keeley." She took two steps backward, giving him two thumbs up and a hesitant smile. "We're good? Right?"

He released the tension in his jaw with a controlled exhale. Why hadn't he fired her by now? "Go get ready." Because he knew she worked harder than anyone else. Once she actually got ready to work.

She bounced on her toes and rushed through the dining room, waving to other waiters and waitresses she passed.

He shifted, slipping his hands into his pockets and tearing his eyes away from her retreating figure. A damn nice figure.

Taking a deep breath, he pushed her out of his mind and observed his waitstaff straightening chairs, ensuring the tables were aligned correctly. The dark wood floors and exposed wood beams gave his restaurant a homey feel, just like the pubs back home, except larger. The rich smell of Irish stew and fresh soda bread made him thankful his younger brother had become a chef. Various pictures of Ireland, green landscapes with gray skies hung on the walls, all artwork he and his brothers had collected over the years.

"Mr. O'Keeley?" Lenny, his shift manager, stopped beside him. "We just received a call for a dinner reservation for forty. Do you want me to open up the long room upstairs?"

"Yes. What's the name on the reservation?"

"Simmons?" Lenny said it like a question. At Brogan's raised eyebrow, Lenny cleared his throat and tilted his chin up. "It's Simmons."

Brogan let a rare smile show. He'd worked with the kid to make sure he came across with authority in his new position as a shift manager. "Good." He started to walk away. Simmons. "Randy Simmons?"

"Yes, sir. Did you still want me to put them in the upstairs room?"

The man had some gall coming into O'Keeley's when he planned to tear it down. "Yes." His eye caught Selena leaving the back storeroom where the employees had a small changing area and break tables. Her hair now in a ponytail was swinging back and forth as she hustled to her area. "Assign Selena to the group."

"But that's past her shift."

Selena might be a mess of a woman, but she could easily handle a large group with a couple of other waiters as support. And she could probably use the tips. "Let me talk to her." He didn't know anything about her personal life. On purpose. He sure as hell didn't need that as a distraction. But, based on her hurried state and constant need to wear flip flops, he assumed she could use the money.

Lenny hesitated long enough to catch Brogan's attention.

"Was there something else, Lenny?"

Lenny cleared his throat. "I was going to offer to work the group too. It's past my shift as well, but if you didn't mind—"

"Are you needing to pick up some extra cash?" The young guy's beat-up car came to mind. Brogan might not have always driven a nice, luxury vehicle, but he kept his possessions as nice as possible. Lenny looked as though he played bumper cars for fun.

"Not exactly." A ruddy color appeared on his cheeks. "I've been trying to find a way to ask Selena out. I thought, maybe, if we worked together on the Simmons' party—"

"Have you lost your mind, boy?" Brogan crossed his arms, belatedly realizing how thick his accent had turned. He didn't know what irritated him more. The fact that Lenny was a supervisor to Selena and that was utterly irresponsible or the thought of his small, wimpy hands pawing all over her body.

"I...I...I," he fumbled.

Brogan narrowed his eyes.

Lenny finally shrugged. "I don't know."

Brogan leaned over, coming within an inch of Lenny's pointy nose. "You are in a supervisory position as a shift manager. You cannot date anyone in this business.

Everyone, including you, signed an employment contract with our sexual harassment clause *highlighted.* It is grounds for immediate dismissal. Do you understand me?"

Lenny's eyes grew round. "Yes, sir."

The first customer opened the door. Brogan straightened and adjusted his tie, addressing the customers with as warm of a smile as he could muster. "Welcome to O'Keeley's."

He turned and walked toward the back of the dining room. He needed a few minutes to himself to come down from the edge of anger. Lenny was young and didn't know the way the professional world worked. He would have to learn it quickly, or he'd find himself out of a job. Some things were intolerable. Especially after four sexual harassment claims that his company had to settle over the past ten years. Three were legitimate claims that he paid the damages and changed his workplace policy because of.

And the one, the most expensive one, had been a charge leveled against him.

He knew himself and his morals. Knew that he'd never, intentionally, pursue a woman inappropriately. But she'd blinded him: pretending to be interested, plotting, executing her plan perfectly, causing their restaurant to settle the claim outside court for half his salary that year. And she'd smiled as she'd walked away.

No woman was worth it. Lenny just didn't know that yet.

"Mr. O'Keeley?" Selena stopped him with a light touch of her hand before he entered his office.

He hadn't noticed her or else he could have ventured a different direction. Avoidance seemed to be his only defense.

"Can you come to look at this?"

"What is it, Selena?" He gritted his teeth against the smooth way her name rolled off his tongue. She didn't seem to notice as she led the way to the back of the restaurant. He'd almost refused to hire her because of his body's uncanny reaction each time she spoke. It'd happened since the very first interview. She'd shown up, wearing a tidy outfit with her hair falling around her shoulders.

Six months later and nothing had changed.

"I wanted your opinion." She stopped by a table and pulled out a chair and sat down. Then stood up. Then sat down.

Brogan crossed his arms. "Getting your workout in?"

She rolled her eyes, a small dimple he'd not noticed before appeared along the corner of her mouth. He'd just gotten done lecturing Lenny about involvement with subordinates, and he seemed to see every little thing about this woman.

She rose again. "Yeah. That would be the first time in a year I've had time to work out. No. The chair feels loose." She pointed to the seat. "Try it."

He gripped the back of the chair and shook it. "It seems fine." He stepped to leave. "I don't have time to play musical chairs. And neither do you."

"And I'm not an idiot." The heat with which she said the words to him made him pause. Her pretty eyes narrowed for a fraction of a second.

"I'm sorry," he said, fascinated by her attempt to get herself under control. He knew the feeling. "I didn't mean it that way."

"Then—" she pressed two fingers to his shoulder, her golden eyes locked with his, "— sit." The sharp demand in her voice seemed to startle her. She snatched her hand away and cleared her throat. "Please."

He sat. At that one moment, she could have told him to bark like a damn dog, and he would've. His gut twisted.

Nerves. Fear. He would not lose his head over an employee again. Not when there were dozens and dozens of beautiful women in Atlanta.

Plenty of other women who weren't employees.

Plenty who wouldn't file a claim against his business. Because with all the other shit thrown at the restaurant lately, that would be the end of O'Keeley's.

The seat of the chair shifted instantly. "I can feel what you mean." Brogan stood, glad to have something to focus on besides his off-limits employee. He flipped the chair upside-down. The chair lacked one screw, causing the entire thing to become unstable. "I'll fix it. Thank you."

She blinked, reminding him of a surprised cat with her eye color. "Oh. You're welcome, Mr. O'Keeley."

For some reason, he didn't like her calling him that. It'd never bothered him before. Everyone called him Mr. O'Keeley. They called his younger brother Chef and his youngest brother, Cathal. The lazy sot didn't get a title.

Taking the chair, he left the dining room, happy to have a few minutes to himself before his brothers arrived for their Monday lunch meeting. They always met on Mondays to accommodate Rian's travel schedule. He'd flew back to Atlanta from wherever he traveled on Sundays. And Cathal, well, Brogan wasn't too sure what the hell Cathal did most of the time besides pick up women and drink whiskey. He occasionally put his degree to use and played lawyer.

After fixing the chair, Brogan tightened his tie and left his office to find Selena. He was still her boss. Even if he didn't want Randy Simmons in his restaurant, the forty-guest party would bring in a good-sized tip.

Lenny stood with an arm propped up on the bar, talking to Selena. He touched her on the shoulder, his hand lingering far too long.

Brogan slowed in his stride. Annoyance and anger flooded through his veins. He couldn't pinpoint what bothered him more. The fact that Lenny was opening himself and the company up for a lawsuit or the fact that Selena might be interested in the little turnip.

Not that Brogan had any interest in making a play for her, but he still hated the thought of another man touching her.

The dark side of his brain didn't give two damns that initiating a personal relationship with her meant trouble. Very expensive trouble.

He'd have to hand it to Lenny, though. The boy knew exactly how to get himself fired.

"Brog," Rian called as he approached from the back hallway. "How's it going?"

Brogan crossed his arms, the suit pulling tight across his back. "I'm trying to figure out why I promoted that piece of shit who's hitting on Selena."

Rian scanned the restaurant. "Selena? Not sure I've met her. Does he not know how it works once you're in a position of power? It puts every female in your business off-limits." He shrugged. "Or male. Can't assume things these days."

"He does as I just laid it out for him not ten minutes ago." Brogan moved toward them as Lenny pulled out his phone. Getting her number? Workplace friendships were fine. What employees on the same level did *outside* of work was their own business. But in his restaurant, during work hours, was his business. His liability. His shitty reminder about how gullible he'd once been.

"Lenny. Selena." Brogan looked between the two of them. "Is there a problem?" His eyes cut back to Lenny. That unattractive red color came back into his skin again as he fumbled with his phone and began to stammer. He'd thought he could teach the boy some managerial skills. But if he were hitting on Selena, he'd be fired before his first paycheck hit the bank.

"Mr. O'Keeley, did you fix the chair?" Selena's gaze held his for a long moment, long enough that he'd almost tuned out the bumbling, incoherent Lenny beside him.

"It's not what it looks like," Lenny finally managed to stammer out. "I wasn't, I mean, she asked me about going to the movies." He nodded his head so vigorously, it might have shaken itself off his shoulders.

At Selena's sharp intake of breath, her eyes widening, Brogan knew the truth. He focused his wrath, and frustration, entirely on Lenny. "Do you want to try that again?"

Lenny's eyes begged Selena to go along with it. It was pathetic if nothing else. Had she really agreed to go on a date with him in the first place? If this was the best Selena could do as far as a date, his impression of American men just sank lower.

Ignoring Lenny for the moment, he faced Selena, blocking Lenny from her view. "Did you ask Lenny on a date?" She opened her mouth and leaned to try and see around Brogan, but he shifted. "You don't need him to answer. Yes or no. Did you ask him out?"

Her tongue darted out, wetting her bottom lip and pulling his attention away from his annoyance for a brief second. He slipped his hands into his pockets to quell the urge to reach out to her.

"No," she whispered so low he almost missed it.

"Did he ask you out?"

Lenny tapped him on the shoulder. "Mr. O'Keeley—"

Brogan held up his hand, and Lenny stopped. Rian sat at

a nearby table. Get the man a bag of popcorn, and he'd have a full show to watch. Rian owned a third of the restaurant. The least he could do, besides create the menu, was to help out with the employee drama. But both his brothers had volunteered Brogan for the position. They argued that he was so used to bossing them around, it was a natural personality trait.

"Yes," Selena whispered even softer. Then she mouthed, "Don't fire him. Please."

He should. Fire him on the spot like he'd done to the employees earlier. Make an example. Why didn't she want him fired, though?

He snapped around to face Lenny. The boy had shifted from a red face to pale. Brogan rolled his eyes. "Don't go fainting on me now." He pulled out a barstool and shoved Lenny into it.

"Please don't fire me. I promise I won't do it again."

"You're right. Starting next week, you will never manage a shift that Selena is working."

Selena set her hand on his arm. His muscles contracted automatically from the contact. Like before when she'd pushed him to sit in the chair, her hands snapped away, and the smallest gasp escaped her lips.

Brogan tilted his head toward her, waiting, wishing she'd touch him again and hating himself for it.

She rubbed the palms of her hands together. "I can't work at night, Mr. O'Keeley."

Again, he wanted to tell her to call him Brogan, but he'd be no better than Lenny. "I know. Lenny will work at night if he wants this job."

Lenny nodded. "Absolutely. Again. I'm sorry."

Brogan shifted to leave, but Selena stood in his way.

"Thank you," she murmured. Her body leaned a fraction

closer, enough, so he smelled a sweet scent that suited her. Sweet like the honey color of her hair. Eyes. Skin.

Back to being in charge and putting a barrier up, he crossed his arms, and his voice deepened. "You can thank me by being on time and ready to work tomorrow." He took two steps toward Rian before stopping. "Oh, and if you want a pretty decent tip, there's a large party coming in at seven. It's yours if you want it."

"Wow. Yeah. Let me see if I can make arrangements." She began to move away but pulled up short. "Do you mind if I go make a few phone calls so I can be free tonight?" She pointed to her section. "No one is in my area yet."

Brogan waved her off. Better she leaves his sight than look at him that way again.

Or move in closer, implying that if he did give her a kiss, she might kiss him back.

As he sat across from Rian, his younger brother smirked. "That was interesting."

"I don't want to talk about it." Because he couldn't explain it. Selena was the most unorganized woman he knew, and for some reason, she still attracted him without doing a damn thing. He didn't really blame Lenny for trying, but he wouldn't foot the bill in the end if things turned south.

He wouldn't risk his brothers' futures. If the three of them didn't raise the money to buy the property, Randy Simmons would come in and level the whole block, evicting them from their space and making them start from scratch somewhere else.

Another costly sexual harassment lawsuit and they'd never reach their goals. Everyone had to play by the rules. Careful and safe. Including himself. He couldn't enforce his own rules while trying to lure the pretty Selena a little closer.

He'd suffer in silence. His brothers wouldn't understand. They knew the first lawsuit, the one Crissy filed against him, was fake. Made-up. And they'd supported him. The same way he'd supported both of them in the past.

He was the oldest. He'd helped take care of his family his entire life, and he'd continue to do so. And that meant no Selena now, or ever.

2

Selena slapped the alarm clock, silencing the overly cheerful radio advertisement for a summer clothing sale she couldn't afford anyway. Waking up at a quarter till six hurt her soul after going to bed at one in the morning. Her feet and back ached from working a twelve-hour shift yesterday. She needed the money, and she was glad Mr. O'Keeley had given her the opportunity, but it'd made for an even longer day. And heftier nurse's bill.

It was hard to tell if she enjoyed the night shift or merely a night off from watching Mimi. She remembered why she enjoyed working from lunch to happy hour most days. She didn't miss what came along with serving jackass men drinking liquor. A few of the men at the Simmons' party got O'Keeley's nice restaurant mixed up with the ones where you hit on the waitresses and called them "sugar" all night.

She walked to her bathroom to start the shower, stubbing her toe and letting as many curse words fly as possible. It usually took away some of the pain as she ended up laughing at her creativity, but after the late night, she couldn't even bring herself to smile. It was going to be one hell of a day.

After a cold shower, because the water heater was out again, she wrapped her hair up in a towel and headed to the kitchen. Mimi would be awake in another hour, wanting her breakfast and maybe, if she was lucky, remembering the current year. Her memory jumped back and forth between the present day and 1946.

Apparently, Selena looked like her great-grandmother because the resemblance was enough to keep Mimi from overreacting when she did have an episode. That was a plus side to her living with Selena, although she couldn't give her the kind of care she really needed.

If the damn insurance company would send someone to spend more than ten minutes with her, maybe she could point it out. There were facilities out there that helped with memory problems. Each day Mimi spent in their cramped apartment was one more day she might lose her memory for good. It's not like she could afford a lawyer to help with her case or to figure out all the paperwork. She could barely afford the nurse.

She cracked eggs for Mimi's breakfast harder than necessary, doubling her frustration with the situation when she had to fish the tiny bits of shell out of the bowl. She didn't have time for this.

"Mama?" Mimi called.

Selena's head dropped. Back to 1946. The morning could get worse. Somehow. She was sure of it. She didn't have time to contemplate how.

After getting breakfast made and cleaned, and Mimi changed into regular clothes, Selena headed to her own room to dress. With thirty minutes until she needed to leave, she pulled the laundry from the dryer and dumped it onto her bed. Selena rummaged through the pile before stepping back into the bathroom. On the floor lay her work shirt, right where she'd stripped out of it before falling into bed – not washed.

They'd given her two when she started, and she'd never bought another one, saving that money instead. She had to run laundry every night for Mimi anyway, might as well wash her work shirt along with it.

Too bad she left her other shirt in the locker at work in case she ever got hers dirty. Mr. O'Keeley dressed impeccably, and she didn't doubt that he wouldn't approve of a member of his staff running around with shepherd's pie spilled down the front of their shirt.

Waking up thinking about her boss was probably a warning sign that her infatuation had gone too far. No denying he was gorgeous. And cultured. Smart. Everything that she wasn't.

But Mr. O'Keeley didn't intimidate her. She refused to let herself be pushed around again. Not after her last, long-term boyfriend hid her away from his high society friends. But she'd been younger then. And she'd wanted to please Jacob.

That felt like a lifetime ago. Now, her mom had taken off with some guy to California, and Mimi was her responsibility. Knowing how to act at a country club or five-star restaurant didn't pay the bills.

"I'll just get there early and change." Pulling on a clean tank top, she headed out of the bedroom, leaving the pile of laundry a complete mess on the bed. But what was new? "I'm going to wait at the door for Ms. Perry."

"Alright, Selena," Mimi cooed in her slow, Southern voice, back in reality and flipping through a catalog that neither one of them could afford a thing from. Mimi had helped raise her, her own father taking off shortly after her ninth birthday. He'd also belonged to a different level of society, according to her mother – one where water heaters didn't stop working every other day.

Selena tapped the screen of her cell phone, staring at the time as she stood at the door to her apartment. Suddenly, she felt a pang of sympathy for what she put Mr. O'Keeley through as she waited for the nurse. "Why couldn't Ms. Perry make it by ten thirty for once in her life?" she muttered.

Finally, the nurse, who might have been a year or two younger than Mimi and moved just as slow, arrived.

"I have to run," she called to Ms. Perry, passing her on the stairs. At this rate, she would be even later than yesterday. Mr. O'Keeley had explicitly asked her to be on time. She was *almost* ready. She might not have on the right shirt, but she did have her shoes and hair fixed for the day. And a little makeup to cover her dark circles.

No way she'd make it there on time.

Selena tore out of the parking lot and cut through a neighborhood to avoid rush hour traffic. After following a school bus which made four stops, she slammed on her brakes and laid on the horn of her small car, hoping to get the dog in the middle of the road to move. It turned its head, staring at her with a pathetic look. The kind of look the dogs on those commercials gave, had her feeling guilty for not having more money to save them all.

The dog moved in slow steps across the rest of her lane. Nope. That dog didn't care that Selena was already twenty minutes late leaving.

But her boss would care.

He'd give her a disapproving kind of look. The one that

made her both want to melt into a puddle and make some smart-ass comment. He was bossy. Rude. Dominating.

And hot.

God, his blue eyes pinned her in place and made her lose track of her thoughts. If only she could figure out a way to have the rest of him pin her down.

She honked again, and the dog picked up speed, trotting to the side of the road, looking like a hitchhiker down on his luck.

She'd been there. Not a hitchhiker, but that depressed, sad state where it felt like a good, substantial meal might change everything. Now, she had a steady job she loved. If she still had the job after showing up late so many times, because, according to Mr. O'Keeley, on time was late.

That saying never made any damn sense to her. But why should it? She was "on time" everywhere she went. She wouldn't go around purposefully late. It wasn't even her fault this morning. It'd rarely been her fault since her grandmother moved in.

Mr. O'Keeley didn't have to worry about things like grandmothers. He probably had "people" to take care of that. His suits screamed money, which was another reason she should stop her dumb daydreams. She didn't know anything about fancy wine or food. Her apartment was a little better than a shit-hole, the best she could afford now supporting her grandmother, whose Social Security checks were split between her expensive medicine and covering part of her nursing care.

Selena had already been in one relationship with a man who cared about money and appearance. And she had no intention of returning.

But her body didn't care about her intentions. It intended to keep right on daydreaming about Mr. O'Keeley and that accent. Especially when he got the least bit irritated, and it dropped a little deeper.

She ran a yellowish red light. Orange. She'd call it an orange light for now and ignore the adrenaline rush at breaking the law. Some things were worth breaking the law. Getting to work on time so your anal-retentive boss didn't fire you was one of them.

Her phone rang, and she answered it, flipping it to speakerphone and setting it in her lap. Hands-free driving was a luxury she didn't have. "I'll be there in ten."

"He's still in his office. I bet if you make it in like five minutes, he wouldn't even know you're late. Again." Katie whispered every word.

"I'll do the best I can."

"You better not get fired. I couldn't stand to work here without you." Katie had become a close friend in the past six months, both starting at O'Keeley's at the same time.

Selena shook her head and blew through another orange light. "You love it there as much as I do."

"I meant about Mr. O'Keeley. He makes me nervous."

He made Selena nervous, too, but based on her tone of voice, not in the same way as Katie. "I'll be there. Bye."

She raced down the street, swinging into the parking lot at a NASCAR pace and pulling her small car into its usual spot. She grabbed her purse and sprinted through the parking lot. The quicker she got into the building, the better. And, as it was every morning she was late, she hoped she didn't see Mr. O'Keeley.

But really, she hoped she did.

Instead of walking through the door at 10:59 a.m., she arrived at a stunning 11:02 a.m. But Mr. O'Keeley didn't wait by the front door as usual. Her luck might have turned around. She booked it through the dining room and straight into the employee break room to change.

Two men turned around as she entered, both smiling in greeting before focusing back to their jobs. Tools and an air compressor sat in the middle of the room as part of the air conditioning unit was dismantled.

Great. Now she had to waste another ten minutes making it to the bathroom across the freaking restaurant and back. And in front of everyone. She wrinkled her nose and glanced at the men in the corner. No. She couldn't change in here.

She stepped into the hallway. Mr. O'Keeley's office sat directly across from the break room, door open, and his desk empty. It would take two seconds to change shirts. Not second-guessing herself, she darted into the empty office and pushed the door closed.

In a world record, she snapped off her pink tank top and slipped into her white work shirt. She unzipped her skinny jeans, tugging them low enough down her hips to get her shirt tucked into them. She turned to leave and froze as her eyes swept the room.

The office wasn't empty.

Three very attractive, very Irish, men watched from a small sitting area off to the side. A large leather sofa and two chairs were angled around a coffee table. Good time to realize the office was more prominent than just a square box and all the owners had decided *that* morning to hold a meeting.

"Sorry?" She winced when her eyes locked with her boss's agitated glare. Of the three men, he was the only one not smiling, which was a good thing. The two times she'd seen him smile had resulted in her physically drooling onto her shirt. She didn't have a spare shirt to change into this time.

"I'd like to introduce Selena Chapman," he said, his flat, even voice laced with disapproval. He could join the club of men who disapproved of her for one reason or another. First, it was her father and then her long-time, now ex-boyfriend. She never truly understood why her father left. Her mother's explanations were always hard to comprehend with half a bottle of vodka in her system. And her ex-boyfriend—well, he left for a very apparent reason. She wasn't good enough.

"Selena, I'm not sure you've met my brothers." They all stood. Mr. O'Keeley, her boss, pointed to one that was barely an inch taller than him but thinner. Like a runner. He wore a black shirt that fit his toned frame with a pair of blue jeans. "This is Rian O'Keeley."

Oh, God. He was a famous chef.

Mr. O'Keeley half-way waved in the direction of the other one, almost dismissively. "Cathal."

Cathal had a devilish smile. Damn. With his looks and presumed Irish accent, women probably threw themselves at him. His blue collared shirt tucked neatly into chinos, hugged his shoulders and highlighted his eyes even from a distance. Did it hurt to be that pretty?

And why, as the other two brothers watched with amusement, did she have to be attracted to the one with the grouchy disposition?

"Unless either one of you would like to take over the employee side of management, do you mind if I have a word with Selena in private?"

Rian held his hands up. "Have at it. I'm going to check the kitchen. Nice to, um, meet you, Selena."

Her face flamed. "You, too." Nothing like showing all

three of your bosses your unsexy white bra before lunch. And underwear. She closed her eyes for a brief second. She'd pulled down her jeans, too.

Cathal didn't budge. He wasn't looking at her; he watched his brother with humor.

"Since that sounds like actual work," he said after the long pause, his accent thicker than the other two, "I think I'll leave you to it."

"Good idea," Mr. O'Keeley answered, crossing his arms the way he always tended to do. His suit jacket was laid over the back of the chair, and white shirt sleeves rolled to his elbows. How could just his tan forearms cut with muscle attract her?

She waited for Cathal to leave and then took one, two steps forward. "I really am sorry." She hitched a thumb over her shoulder. "There were two men in the break room fixing the air conditioner, and I thought I could slip in here and change so I can put my tank top back in the locker room and not have to make two trips, one to the bathroom and one back to put my shirt up. I wanted to start work as soon as possible without calling a bunch of attention to myself." She bit her bottom lip as he watched her another moment in silence. She'd caused herself too much attention already.

"About that. We need to talk about your timeliness."

The air in her body rushed out. Now was the point where he fired her. She'd held this job for six months, longer than the others. And she liked it. She was good at it. Not having a college degree limited her choice of employment. And men. Jacob had made that clear enough. Sophisticated men like her boss, who reminded her of an angry bull at the moment, didn't date girls from the other side of the tracks which might embarrass them. She'd embarrassed her ex enough times to learn that lesson the hard way.

But her boss didn't want to date her. He wanted to fire her. She would not let that happen without a fight.

"Please, don't fire me. I really need this job."

"I want you to try and be here by nine thirty in the morning from now on."

"Nine thirty?" He didn't want to fire her? She thought about the extra forty dollars for the cost of the nurse. Could she pull that off with her budget?

"Yes. That way, you might get here by eleven." He smirked. And damn if that wasn't just as sexy. "I'll pay you for the time that you're here. If you show up before your shift starts, then you'll help where needed to prep for the day. Full wage, not as a waitress."

"How much?"

Now that she was openly staring at her sexy boss, she realized his nose was a little crooked like it'd been broken once or twice. Probably some uptown accident. There was no way Mr. O'Keeley would lower himself to an actual fight. He was too high-class for that. Might get his perfectly pressed suit wrinkled. Or mess up his neatly combed dark brown hair.

"Twenty-five."

She hadn't expected that. "You'll pay me an extra twenty-five dollars to get here an hour earlier?"

"Technically, if you got here on time, you'd be here an hour and a half before your shift. Consider it an incentive. I don't want to have to fire you, Selena. You're a great waitress. Efficient. Professional." His lips kicked to the side again, and he looked away. "When you keep your shirt on."

She'd embarrassed him. The thought of anyone, even a woman in a crappy white bra, flustering the stoic, high-class Mr. O'Keeley amused her. She'd never been on that side of the equation before.

"You have a deal. And I'll be sure not to take my shirt off again in your presence." Her mouth would forever get her in trouble. She'd meant it as a joke. The whole, laughing with someone instead of laughing *at* someone. He didn't seem to take it that way.

His blue eyes locked onto her for one long beat of silence, enough for her to know that underneath that hard, shell exterior, something ran hot and dangerous. Maybe she shouldn't joke with her boss, especially since they didn't even have the outside chance at a relationship—even a one-night relationship.

Her employment contract prevented that by her agreeing to the no dating clause. He'd fired two employees just yesterday. And based on the way he'd chided and almost fired Lenny, Mr. O'Keeley reaffirmed that he didn't play around when it came to the rules.

He cleared his throat. "How did last night go?"

"Last night? Oh. The party of forty. It went well. They all seemed to enjoy the food." She thought back to the two men who'd slipped her their phone numbers. Creeps.

"Did you hear any of their conversation at the table?"

She stuck her hands in her back pockets, trying to appear relaxed. She had heard their conversation, but until then, she'd forgotten.

"Yes. They were talking about a development. Real estate, I imagine. I know Atlanta has plenty of places to shop, but I don't live too far from here, so putting in a Big Jim's Superstore in downtown Atlanta works nicely for me. Do you know where?"

"Here."

She chewed on her lip a moment. "Here? As in—"

"The developers are planning to purchase this entire block of buildings and make it into your superstore." He snarled as he said it, his Irish so thick, she had a hard time understanding him.

"Great." She threw her hands in the air. Finally found a job that could cover the nurse's bill *and* buy groceries and she might lose it anyway.

"I'm glad you're happy about it."

She cut her eyes his way. "I was being sarcastic, Mr. O'Keeley."

"Brogan."

Her breath froze in her lungs.

"Call me Brogan when we aren't around the other employees. Mr. O'Keeley feels too formal."

He'd said nothing improper for a boss. No insinuations. He hadn't moved any closer to her, she'd moved closer to him, if anything, but it felt intimate calling him by his first name.

When you flash someone your bra, it must drop you down to a first name basis. Did other employees call him Brogan when they were in private?

She licked her dry lips and hoped she played it off smoothly. "Alright, Brogan." The dark blue of his eyes seemed to deepen the longer he watched her. "What do you plan to do about the development?"

He began rolling down his shirtsleeves. "I'm not sure yet. That was the meeting that you pleasantly interrupted. The owner of this building gave me the first right of refusal. But the asking price is more than we can afford at the moment. We don't have much leverage to put up. I've reinvested almost everything back into the business."

She pressed her lips together to keep her mouth from dropping open. He was talking to her. Like a human and not just an employee. "Oh. So, I really might be out of a job after all?"

He buttoned his cuffs, looking sexier than any boss should. God, she should look away. It seemed personal, watching him dress. But, hell, he'd just watched her dress, and it'd been a little more revealing than him covering up those amazing arms.

"I hope that doesn't happen, but I won't lie to you. That is a possibility. But as of right now at 11:25 a.m. you do have a job. And so do I." He slipped into his jacket. His tie sat a little crooked.

He walked toward her, a natural smile she'd never seen before in place. Real. Open. The kind of smile that makes you feel like you are the center of that person's universe for that one moment.

He motioned toward the door of his office. "Shall we?"

Out of nowhere, she reached up, adjusted his tie. She never understood why her body didn't listen to her rational mind. He'd given her permission to use his first name.

Not touch him.

Not skim the tip of her finger along the edge of his collar against his smooth skin.

And, judging by the mask that fell over his beautiful face again, he didn't appreciate it.

She stepped back. "Sorry. I know you wouldn't want to go out there with a crooked tie."

"No, I wouldn't." His expression didn't match that husky, sexy quality that'd slipped into his voice. Maybe she'd imagined it. Sophisticated men like Brogan never looked twice at women like her. Or if they did, it was for a fling. Nothing serious.

Jacob had dated her longer than what she'd describe as a fling, but it didn't change anything in the end. He wanted someone who could make the rounds at his fancy parties. Host dinners for other uppity men and women. And when he discovered she wasn't the "right" woman, he'd hid her away.

"Then let's go to work." She turned on her heel and marched out ahead of him, swinging close to the break room door long enough to throw her tank top in the general direction of her locker. Neatness be damned. She had a job to do while there was still an O'Keeley's open.

"Do you normally throw your clothes around?" He'd waited for her in the hallway, the expression from before a little less severe.

She smiled over her shoulder as they headed out into the main dining room, already partially full, from the downtown lunchtime crowd. "I do when I strip for my boss." That was another mark against her dating someone like Brogan or Jacob. Her sarcasm was hardly tolerated. Or appreciated.

But Brogan didn't chastise her.

He grinned.

And she about tripped over her own feet.

"Go to work, Selena," he said, a definite edge of laughter in his beautiful voice.

Risking even more mortification. "You, too—" she winked "—Brogan."

3

Two miles in the pool should have cooled off his body. Eased his mind. Settled the swirling deep in his gut that hadn't stopped. But with each flip-turn in the water, some part of Selena popped into his mind. Her eyes. That damn wink. The way she'd skimmed her jeans down her hips.

He pushed harder until his watch buzzed an hour later.

She was due at the restaurant in forty-five minutes, so he'd head straight into work from the gym. They'd renovated the office, giving him his private changing area as well as a separate area for the employees. His space included a shower.

Maybe, after a shower and putting on his suit, his control would return. Usually, his two-hours of morning exercise gave him a chance to work through problems. One big problem staring him down at the moment was what to do about his restaurant and the offer to buy the property.

Three million dollars. He didn't have the collateral to get that type of loan without more time and planning. He and his brothers worked hard to be successful since leaving

Ireland fifteen years ago—from a small goat farm and fighting at the local pub to running a business. They all had their parts to play.

Right now, Cathal was in charge of all the legal business concerning the purchase of the property. Somehow, Georgetown had given the man a damned law degree. His brother was smart. Stupid smart. The kind of intelligence that made you cringe when he showed up scuttered every other night hitting on anything in a skirt.

Opposite from Rian. Although, Rian was an odd one himself. Quiet. A genius in the kitchen. He'd spend his time traveling the world, cooking for famous people or showing off his skills at culinary festivals rather than put down solid roots.

Brogan dried off and pulled on his t-shirt and a dry pair of gym shorts. Both his brothers had their ghosts that they ran from. He knew that. It didn't make it any easier when he was trying to keep their restaurant running.

His ghosts arose each time he had to look, touch, smell Selena, and then walk away. A hot shower and shave would put him into the frame of mind he needed to deal with the day.

To handle Selena.

After the first harassment lawsuit and payout, he never looked twice at an employee. Never crossed a line. Wouldn't. Even if his mind and his eyes always drifted back to Selena. He preached it enough to his employees. Lenny almost had a date with Brogan's fist had he not looked so shaken from the encounter and backed off.

But he didn't blame the boy. Selena was gorgeous, in a messy way. He believed organization led to success, so being late and unprepared almost every day would drive him insane. That was a good enough reason for him to stay away from her.

So, why in the hell had he told her to show up early? That put them together, alone, at least thirty minutes before the cooks arrived. They were both responsible adults. He'd make sure to keep everything professional and keep his distance. Then she couldn't accuse him of anything.

He walked the few blocks to the office from the gym, unlocking the door, and disarming the beeping alarm panel. This was what he needed. A big reminder as to where to focus his mind. O'Keeley's.

"Good morning!"

He whipped around, barely catching the door before it closed in Selena's face. "Hi, there." He glanced at his watch. Not too early, but 9:15 a.m. was incredibly early for her.

"I know. Sorry, I'm early." Her eyes tracked down his body and back up. "You're not in a suit." She blinked like she was shocked. "I can wait outside."

He shook his head. "No. Come in. I just need to get cleaned up from the gym, is all. How did you manage to get here by 9:15 a.m.?"

"It seems that my mornings work a little better, leaving earlier."

He wanted to ask, "Why," but he kept the question to himself. That was her business. Not his. He pointed down to her feet. "You even have your shoes on."

"I figured you'd notice. But you probably notice everything." She sighed. "I'm too overwhelmed to remember anything without writing it down." They stopped in the hallway between his office and the break room. "So, where do we start."

"The shower."

Her laugh was quick and loud. "I've already taken mine, but thanks for the invite."

He winced. That was a *great* way to keep everything professional. "No. Sorry. I meant I need to take a shower." Now he was acting like an idiot. "If you want to you can do a walkthrough, double-check things. I won't be long." A cold shower to clear his head.

"Sure thing." She walked to her locker, her shoulder barely visible from the door to his office. He had to get his mind under control. Because in that one second, he pictured her in the shower.

With him.

Which would never happen. He'd have a lawsuit handed to him quicker than he could get lathered up for a shave.

He showered and shaved in record time, ready to go over the tedious paperwork, as his brothers called it, and distract himself from the pretty waitress currently walking through the dining room.

"I did the walk-through—" Selena's voice trailed off. She stood in the doorway. They weren't alone in the building any longer; the cook's already prepping for the day in the kitchen, which was a good thing with the way her gaze held his.

"What is it?"

"You look different. Without a tie and your sleeves rolled up."

He smiled. "I hate ties."

She crossed her arms and leaned on the doorjamb. "Really? I would have thought you slept in a suit."

"Not until I'm six feet under, I'm afraid."

"Then why wear one?" She tilted her head to the side. "You run an Irish pub. And you're the boss. You make the rules."

"I run a business." And as a new kid out of college, no one took him seriously. The suit added an element of power that he leveraged. Still did. So did making rules and sticking to them.

She stood there, watching him. Thinking. He could tell when she thought hard about something because her lips pursed together and distracted the hell out of him.

"I still need something else to do."

"Right." He motioned to the seat across from him. "I was wondering how you were with a computer?"

"Decent." She sat down in the seat he'd indicated. "Why?"

He turned a second, large monitor so she could see it too. "I need someone to go through the review sites. You know, the ones that the tourists use to figure out where to eat. We're trending fairly well, but I want to know what the overall thoughts are. Any simple improvements we can make. See if there's a pattern to what people like or dislike."

She scowled. "You know some people are just plain cruel, right?"

"Yes. I do. Are you afraid I'll get my feelings hurt?"

She pursed her lips together for a moment. "Until I saw you this morning dressed like a normal person in gym clothes, I wasn't sure you had feelings." She waved her hand in the air, her eyes wide. "Never mind. Pretend I didn't say that. Sorry, Mr. O'Keeley."

"I asked you to call me Brogan." And he had feelings. Far too many inappropriate ones aimed her way.

"Sorry. Brogan."

"And can you stop apologizing." He held a finger up. "Except when you're late."

"Are you never late?"

"No."

"Ever?"

He shook his head. "No. It's almost time for the other waitstaff to arrive. If you think this is something you can handle, we can start tomorrow morning. Do you have a laptop?"

She fidgeted in the seat. "No," she finally said, embarrassed. "If I need to buy one—"

"No. I'll give you a company one for you to use. Not a problem." Once he went out and purchased a company laptop. He'd make Cathal do it. "But you can share this one or use my phone until then."

"Okay." She rose. "I know you don't want me to apologize again, but really, I'm sorry about the feelings comment." With a shy smile, she took a step backward. "You just, you know. You look a little more—"

At her long pause, Brogan crossed his arm. "Spit it out, Selena."

"You look a little more human. Like this. Without the tie or jacket." Then she left.

Brogan leaned back in his seat. Human? Oh, if she only knew exactly how human he was underneath his suits. Especially when it came to her.

But humans were flawed. They made mistakes. Lapses in judgment. He wouldn't do that with Selena. Not while she was an employee.

"HOLY SHIT." Katie, platinum hair with newly dyed blue tips pulled back into a ponytail, nudged Selena. "Look at how the boss man is dressed."

Selena's head whipped around; her mouth instantly ran dry. He'd left the tie and jacket in his office. His shirt sleeves were rolled to just below his elbow like earlier. The top button of his shirt undone. Was it because of what she'd said?

"Girl—" Katie pretended to faint. "I'd let that man do almost anything he wanted to me. Anywhere." She laughed. "Based on your face, you're in complete agreement. Oh, shit, he's coming this way."

Katie continued clearing off a table.

Selena didn't move, even knowing her boss had a scowl aimed her way. Her breath quickened with each one of his long, sure steps. Perfect. Brogan was the ideal specimen of a man. Too bad he probably dated models and sophisticated women who wouldn't embarrass him.

"Selena," he began, her name a grumble in his accent that she loved. "Two things. One, I, uh, found your cell phone." He held it out. Had she left it in his office?

"Awesome. Thanks."

"Typically, I'd ask you to keep it in your locker, but—"

Selena held up her hand, stopping him and smiling wide. "I know the rules, boss. What was the second thing you needed to tell me?"

"Lenny won't be in today."

"Did you go ahead and switch him to the night shift?"

"No. I fired him."

Katie gasped and stepped right back to her spot beside Selena. "Seriously? It was because of Lauren, wasn't it? I knew it. There's no way a woman that hot would pursue someone like Lenny." Her voice dropped. "Did you catch them in the supply closet, too?"

Brogan looked confused and annoyed at the same time. "What? Lauren? What happened with Lauren?"

Selena answered to put him out of his misery. "She asked Lenny out on a date and then asked for better tables.

She told me it worked, too. I didn't know if you knew about it or not. Plus, you know, I'm not a snitch."

He ran a hand over his face. "I feel like I'm dealing with high schoolers."

Selena arched an eyebrow. "Present company excluded, I'm sure."

Katie giggled beside her. It was a little presumptuous to assume that they had some type of hesitant friendship, but still, she was twenty-eight. She didn't want to be lumped in with the hormonal drama.

Brogan's scowl darkened. "He was fired for stealing money. I just ran over the video from the bar last night."

"Dang," she mumbled, shaking her head. "I would have never guessed he'd have the balls to do that." She clasped a hand over her mouth. Exhibit "A" as to why she'd never fit in with high society. "Sorry!"

Katie nudged her. "Way to go. You'll be next on the chopping block."

But Brogan seemed amused and not upset. Her ex-boyfriend would have frowned and scolded her like a little child.

"I can't vouch for the size of his anatomy." Brogan crossed his arms. "It does leave us in a bind. I'd hoped to train someone else for his position. To train you, actually. Can you take over his position as shift manager?"

"When?"

"Now."

"Me?"

She looked to Katie, who nodded. "Yes, she can."

"Thank you, Katie," Brogan said. "But I'd like to hear Selena's answer."

"I...I can. If you think I'd be good at it."

Brogan smiled. A full-fledged, outright, sexy as hell smile. Katie sighed and leaned against Selena's shoulder.

Selena managed not to let her knees grow too weak to stand. Yes. He was absolutely the perfect man. Well, aside from his stiff personality.

"I think you'll do just fine. I won't even make you wear a suit."

Was that an attempt at sarcasm? "Thank you."

He looked at Katie and frowned. "Is this your section?"

She squeaked and scurried away, glancing back once before rushing to her area.

"See, you don't need a suit to show people you're in charge," Selena said. Their new relationship, friendship, whatever it was sent butterflies soaring through her body.

Brogan had fired employees each time they started a relationship at the restaurant. He sure as hell wouldn't pursue something with an employee.

He pulled at his already loosened collar. "I had someone tell me I wasn't a human. I'd hate for my employees to think I'm not a fun, likable fellow."

"Look at that. No tie and you're mingling with the little people." She laughed at his scowl. "What about my area if I'm taking over for Lenny?"

"I already called Trey into work. He's wanted to get on the early shift for the past few weeks."

Great. Trey might not ask her out on dates like Lenny but discussing his video games was almost as bad. Good thing she was at a management level now. It gave her a great excuse to stay busy and away from him.

"Thank you again, Brogan."

His eyes softened, the blue bright and offset against his perfectly styled dark hair. "You're welcome. Especially since I just bumped up your morning time to nine."

"Nine?"

"I still need help with those reviews." He leaned toward her. The smell of his woodsy cologne drew her closer, but she managed to keep her place. Nothing screamed management material like sniffing her boss in the middle of the restaurant.

"I have a meeting with the bank in an hour. You'll be in charge. Once Trey arrives, I need you to keep your phone with you and call me if you have any problems." He lowered his voice, his Irish accent deepening. "I'll call you to check in on the restaurant."

"I don't have your number." This was really happening. Instead of dreaming about Brogan from a distance, now she had to figure out how to work with the man, side-by-side. It was like one-sided foreplay.

But, damn, she'd take it over nothing.

"I sent you a text, so you have it now."

Of course, he'd already texted her. Always efficient. She pulled out her phone from her back pocket.

This is Brogan.

It made her smile. Simple and to the point.

He waited a brief moment as if he might add to it, but then turned and walked away, disappearing back into his office, only to reappear fully dressed in his suit and a leather folder in his hand. He took long strides out of the restaurant without giving her a second glance.

Did he realize that every female, literally, she scanned the room, every *single* female in the place watched him leave? Probably. His brother Cathal was obvious about his attraction to and from women. She could tell that from their quick meeting. She wasn't sure about Rian. Although he was as good looking, he seemed more modest. Quiet.

Katie squealed and grabbed her arm. "I think our boss

has a thing for you! He's never talked to anyone else like that. He actually smiled."

She shook her head. "No, he doesn't. Have you forgotten how much of a stickler for the rules he is? He fired two people just this week and almost fired Lenny when he asked me out. He's just friendly because he wants me to do this job. He'd never date an employee. Besides, he hasn't said one thing that would make me think that." Except for the shower comment that morning. But really, anyone could slip up. And if he'd meant it—then she'd missed her opportunity because thinking of him in the shower brought a rush of heat to her cheeks.

"Nope. He is *so* into you," Katie said.

"He scowled at me and gave me more work." If Katie would drop it, maybe Selena could too. She would only drive herself crazy wishing something would happen between them. Because, no matter who it was, her boss, a guy at a bar, she didn't have room to date. Mimi had her complete devotion at this point. No man would take on both of them.

Katie rolled her eyes. "You are so boring. When was the last time you actually went out with a man?"

"Like a serious date? Mimi came to live with me a year ago. So, a year ago." She pressed her lips together, making her brain come up with a good, rational comment about Brogan. "He told me yesterday that he thought I was a good waitress. I swear that's his only interest in me."

"Yeah, but other people have been here longer." Katie's brown eyes shined with excitement.

Selena took Katie by the shoulders. "My first direction to you as your immediate manager is going to be to keep your mouth shut. Brogan—"

"Oh. My. God. You call him Brogan now?"

Shit. "No. I don't. It just slipped out. I met all of the owners yesterday morning when I was late, and in my head, it's hard to call them all Mr. O'Keeley."

Katie made a noise that implied she didn't agree. "I haven't met all the owners. Sounds like special treatment."

She'd never live it down if she'd told her what she did to meet them. "*Mr. O'Keeley* will fire me if he thinks people are gossiping about the two of us. Nothing is going on. I promise. I'm still completely single and just as sexually frustrated as I was two days ago."

Did Brogan actually have relationships? It seemed like his natural authority would overpower someone who wasn't prepared to stand up to him. But then, he probably wouldn't like a woman like that. Why in the world was she even contemplating it?

Katie grabbed her hand. "Then let's go out tonight and celebrate your promotion."

"I don't have the money. You know that."

"My treat. We'll go out, meet some cute guys, maybe girls in my case, have them buy us drinks. Then declare we're really lovers and leave together. It'll be fun. C'mon." Katie cut her eyes at her. "I can get my sister to watch your grandmother. For free. She owes me a favor. It's Thursday night. You know the bars will be full."

A night out sounded fun. Katie's sister was in nursing school. Besides, it was only for a couple hours.

"I see you've already made up your mind." Katie danced in a little circle. "I'll pick you up at ten thirty."

"I need to be back by midnight." She had an early morning date with her boss.

4

"Now, where have you been hiding that adorable waitress?" Cathal O'Keeley leaned back in the chair at the bank, completely relaxed even though they'd been kept waiting for nearly an hour and the fate of their restaurant rested on securing this loan. Not much made Cathal upset. Well, maybe if the local bar ran out of whiskey.

Brogan narrowed his eyes. He'd avoided both his brothers after Selena's incident in his office the day before. And now, he had her phone number in his phone, and that made him nervous. He kept his voice even. "I haven't been hiding her. If you got your sorry ass out of bed before noon and came into the restaurant more often, you wouldn't have to ask me that." He leaned a little closer. "Besides, you know she's off-limits so wipe that dopey smile off your face."

Cathal, unconcerned, shrugged. "I know the rules, dear brother, but judging by your reaction to her little show yesterday morning, I'm wondering if you remember them."

"I didn't have any reaction except the urge to yank your tongue out when it rolled out of your mouth."

"I'd like to see you try." He poked Brogan's arm. "You have all these muscles, and yet I think I could still whip you in a fight."

Rian laughed, soft and low. "Please, Cathal. Not here. Last time you dared him, you broke his nose, and he bruised your ankle so bad you limped for a week. And that was just last year." He ran a hand over his chin. "But he has a point. You did get a certain *look* on your face, Brog."

"Mortification?" Brogan offered. If his brothers knew what rolled through his mind, they would have already beaten him. He wouldn't act on his attraction to Selena. He could maintain a business relationship with her. He'd proved that this morning. She could help the business *and* be on time. He wouldn't call it easy, but it was possible.

Cathal shook his head. "No. Wrong again, dear brother. I know you. You wouldn't have watched it. You would have been a gentleman and said something to her. Looked away. Acted within the square box of your strict rules. Instead, you sat there, dumbfounded."

"I wasn't exactly expecting Selena to march into my office and start stripping." But now that she had, he still couldn't get the memory out of his mind. And she'd promised to never take her shirt off in front of him again – damn shame.

Cathal leaned forward until Brogan glanced his direction. "I think I can speak for Rian when I say that neither one of us have a problem with it."

"With what?"

"With you getting to know the pretty waitress. It's been a long time since you've looked twice at someone who didn't act as stuck up as you do most of the time," Rian said. His smile widened at Brogan's sharp look. "Underneath all your bossy perfection, you want the same thing Ma and Da had.

Someone to sit with you at night, stare at the fire, and be content. That's why none of your other girlfriends ever amounted to anything. You tried to fit into their fancy world, and it didn't work. It will never work for you."

"And you think Selena is that person?" Ridiculous. Neither one of them knew a thing about her. Brogan inferred more than he actually knew. She seemed nice, had made a few friends at the restaurant, and could stop his heart just by straightening his tie.

"She seems down to earth enough that it might be worth a shot," said Cathal.

The door opened, the loan officer walked in and sat down, looking as though he had bad news. "I'm afraid we can't approve the loan. It's just too risky for that amount." He handed Cathal the paper he held. "Your application didn't put any property up for collateral. Do you have any?"

Rian leaned forward. "There's the property back in Ireland."

"No," Brogan said. He wouldn't give up their family land. His parents might be gone, both having died ten years apart, but that was still home, no matter how long he lived in America.

"Thank you for your time. We'll let you know if the situation changes." Cathal shook the man's hand and then motioned for them to leave.

"We aren't putting the land up as collateral," said Brogan as they walked through the lobby. He wouldn't let them. He'd find another way. They weren't risking their last connection to home. If he lost the restaurant, he needed a place to crawl back to.

Cathal shook his head and opened the door to the bank. "Do you ever stop bossing us around?"

Rian answered. "No. He won't. It's like breathing to him.

Always in charge." He held up his hand before Brogan could snap back. "Let me go to Ireland. See what equity we can pull off the land. I need to fly there anyway."

Brogan had headed up their family since their Da died. He'd been fourteen and took on the responsibility. His brothers were more than capable of making their own decisions now. Well, Rian was. The jury was still out on Cathal.

"Fine," he grumbled, hating to give up the control. Asking about the equity in the land wasn't signing away their ownership.

THE LAST STOP was a bar at the end of a block of nightclubs and a few open-late diners. Not many people made it down this far, keeping the crowd at the bar light. That suited Selena just fine. She already regretted coming out with Katie. Her mind still reeled from her interaction with Brogan. She'd rather stay home and daydream of him than make small talk with strangers looking for a quick hook up.

"Let's take a lap around the bar first. Scope everything out before we find a place to post up." Katie linked arms with Selena. "Particularly, scope all the guys out first."

"You've settled for guys tonight?"

"Yeah. You're not the best wingwoman to pick-up women. You're too much competition."

Selena laughed. "Sorry. And I'll follow your lead, but I don't want to walk around too much. You parked like a mile away, I swear. My feet are already killing me." Selena scrunched her toes around in her black stilettos. The idea of finding a guy to take her mind off Brogan interested her, but not at the expense of permanently damaging her feet.

"You look nice." Katie squeezed her tighter. "I might have to take you home myself later."

"I'm not that easy. Not unless you buy me a drink. I want something pink and yummy." Selena never got a night off. And with Katie driving, she could relax. Let down her hair, literally. It fell in loose waves around her shoulders. With her strapless pink dress, it brushed against her skin with each step.

Selena didn't frequent bars every weekend. And, until her recent break-up, Katie didn't either. But going out was a nice reminder that life consisted of more than work and taking care of Mimi.

The tight pink dress had been Katie's idea. One look at Selena's knee-length, black cocktail dress, and Katie had forced her back inside to change. The too-small shoes were her idea as well.

"Oh, that guy at the bar is already watching you." Katie led her along. "Don't look. We'll circle around. Dang, he's staring hardcore. He's gorgeous."

"Maybe he's watching you and not me."

"Please. I know when a guy is looking at me." Katie stood a little straighter. "Like the man over there."

"In the army hat?" Selena grimaced. "No. I don't trust a guy that won't take his hat off to come to a bar like this. It'll be like those country music singers. They're all hot on stage, but then you see them in real life, and it's like, 'no, please, put your hat back on.'"

They both laughed and kept walking until they came back to the end of the bar. Katie kept her promise and bought her a drink. That turned into two drinks. And three.

"I should probably stop at three," Selena announced, not sure what drink the bartender handed her. "I still have to get up early."

Katie shook her head. "I didn't buy you that one. The man watching you bought you that one."

Selena kept her head down as the man in question moved their way. She'd not taken a good look at him, and now she felt a little sleazy for accepting the drink. Whatever it was. It definitely wasn't pink.

"I hope you like whiskey."

She snapped her head up at the Irish accent.

Cathal O'Keeley.

Her eyes widened. Wasn't he like her boss, too?

He chuckled. "Don't look so mortified. I'm not here to get you drunk and take you home. Brogan would have my head for that."

Katie leaned forward. "Brogan? Like our boss, Brogan?"

"Katie, this is Cathal O'Keeley. He's part-owner of the restaurant." The door opened. Great. "And there's the other one."

"Dang. Two hottest guys in the place and they're off-limits. The night is officially a bust."

Selena glanced at her friend, who swayed as she surveyed the crowd. Drunk. When had Katie gotten drunk? She rolled her eyes. There went her ride home. She should have known better.

"I take that back. I'm going to hit on army guy, after all. I'll deal with the hat consequences later." She patted Selena on her knee. "I'll text you if I need saving."

Selena tapped her phone sitting on the bar. "Got it."

"Now," Cathal began, setting both his forearms on the bar and tilting his head to the side. "Why is a woman like you in a place like this?"

"Don't believe a word he says." Rian sat down on the other side of her. Great. Flanked on either side by the brothers of the man she couldn't stop fantasizing about. "Hi, Selena."

"Hi. I'm not sure what to call you. Either one of you, actually."

"Not Mr. O'Keeley," Rian said. "We let Brogan have that title. Rian is fine."

Selena picked up the whiskey drink, holding it up and looking at the contents, keeping her hands busy.

Cathal motioned to the glass. "I didn't drug you if that's what you're wondering."

"No!" She shook her head. "I wouldn't think that. I'm trying to figure out what it is without looking like an idiot." At his bland expression, she smiled. "I guess I already did that, huh?"

"That is a Salt and Honey. It's with Irish whiskey. Try it."

"I might as well. With Katie drunk, I'm afraid I'll have to call a cab at this point anyway." Because as much as she'd like to find a guy to take her mind off Brogan, she didn't want anyone else. Pathetic.

"Alone?" Rian's eyes pulled down tight. He slipped out his phone. "That's not very safe."

"I wasn't supposed to go home alone. At least that wasn't our plan." She took a sip of the drink. "Wow, that's smooth."

Rian watched her with a curious expression. "I didn't peg you for a woman that went out on the prowl."

"Out on the—no. No. That's not me. Definitely not." She waited while he typed into his phone. She took another sip of her drink. He flattered her if he honestly thought she could walk into a bar and walk out with a guy. She'd never done that before. Never had the pleasure of being that irresponsible.

Cathal motioned to the crowd. "Did you find anyone that you fancy?"

She swung around, surveying the guys in the room. Both men turned to face away from the bar as well, their shoulders brushing hers on both sides. Her body didn't react the same as it did with Brogan. Nothing. Even with a fourth drink half-empty.

"What about that guy? He's tall and good looking." Cathal shrugged at her giggle. "I have to size up the competition."

"Oh, please. I promise that this is *not* a come-on, at all, but Katie was right, you really don't have competition in this room." She sent Rian a sideways glance. "You either." She'd probably hate herself in the morning for having said that, but at the moment, she didn't care. The glory and horror of alcohol loosening a tongue. As long as she kept all her sexy thoughts about their brother inside her brain, maybe she'd make it out not completely mortified.

"I'm sure our competition will come walking through that door in about six minutes." Rian folded his hands in his lap. "But, if I wasn't here, that man seems fine."

Selena shrugged, glad for the distraction away from Brogan. Because no one in the room, or the city, compared to Brogan. The man Rian motioned toward spotted her watching him and lifted his hand, waving to Selena. She waved back, a small smile plastered to her lips. "I talked to him earlier. His hands were small."

"Small?" Cathal smirked. "Alright. You're a hard woman to please. What about him?"

She wrinkled her nose. "No. I don't think so. Fake tan. That means he already spends more money on himself with a beauty regimen than I do. My turn. What about that woman over there? Does she strike your *fancy*?"

"She has a nice face. But she's with four other women."

Rian chuckled but didn't add to his brother's observation.

"So? She has friends. Not many women will venture out to a bar by themselves."

"Women who travel in packs that size are hard to separate. They want you to sit down at the table. Talk to all of them. Make all of them feel important. I'm afraid I'm not up for that tonight. I've talked too much today as it is." Cathal's explanation made sense, but it still wasn't fair to women who didn't want to venture out alone.

Rian accepted a pint of beer from the bartender. "Do you want another drink, Selena?"

She blinked, trying to clear the buzzing feeling in her head. Cathal's comment about talking too much reminded her of where they went.

"That's right. You all met at the bank today. How did that go? Your brother told me about needing to find a loan to buy the property."

Rian looked back to the door and back to her. "Not so good. I'm leaving for Ireland soon to talk to our banker over there. See what strings they can pull on the property we still own."

"But Brogan's not leaving?" Could she call him by his first name to his brothers?

Maybe not by the way Rian smiled at her. "No. You probably already know that I travel. A lot."

Cathal finished whatever he'd had in his glass. "Me, I'm okay to fly once or twice, but not keen to do it and work at the same time. Brogan hates airplanes." He pointed at her drink. "Was it good?"

She squinted one eye closed and looked at the glass. "A little too good, I'm afraid."

"Your Katie found herself a man, I see."

Katie had wrapped her arms around the army man, kissing him quite enthusiastically. She did manage to get the hat off since she now wore it – oldest trick in the book.

"I don't know what to do about her. We were supposed to go home together."

Rian chuckled, and Cathal's eyebrows raised higher than she thought possible. She nudged him with her shoulder. "Not like that. Although, I do know Katie loves all people, as she says it. She told me the plan was to tell any guys we meet that we were going home together to get out of the situation." She motioned to her dress. "Despite my appearance, I have to go home soon. Alone."

"And Katie was your driver." Cathal put his arm along the bar behind her back, shifting a little closer.

"Yes. She was."

"I called you a ride." Rian clicked his beer glass to her empty one.

A shadow blocked out the low light above them.

Selena looked up.

Brogan.

"I guess I know why you're always late to work." His gruff voice sent a shiver down her body.

"Give her a break," Cathal said, his arm slipping onto her shoulder and giving her a gentle squeeze. It was brotherly to her, but to Brogan, his eyes narrowed into slits. "She was unwinding after the hard day of work you put her through."

"I'm sorry. You really shouldn't have come down here." She cut her eyes at Rian. He held up his hands in fake innocence. "I'm here with Katie. She's my ride."

Brogan scanned the room. "She's the one currently wearing the army hat and taking shots at the bar."

"Yeah." She waited until he looked back down at her. "She's a pretty shitty DD."

Both Rian and Cathal laughed. Brogan did not.

"Hey there." The man that had waved to her a few moments earlier stepped up beside Brogan, his soft brown eyes were hopeful. "I'd hoped I could buy you a drink?"

She wrinkled her nose, ignoring Brogan's sharp look. "I think I've had enough for the night."

"How about a dance?"

"I really don't think so."

But the man would not be deterred. "We could always get out of this place."

Brogan shifted, blocking the man from Selena's line of sight. "Are you interested in talking to him?"

Part of her wanted to say, "yes," just to see what Brogan would do. But, honestly, she didn't want to talk to anyone but her grumpy, sexy boss. She reached out and nudged Brogan to the side.

"I'm sorry. I think I'm about to leave for the night." Because planned or not, that fourth drink was starting to get to her.

The guy moved away, and Brogan continued to aim his frown at her. "How drunk are you?" He asked her before swinging his gaze to his brothers. "And how much have you two contributed to it?"

Rian took a sip of his beer. "Ask Cathal. I got here a few minutes ago."

"I bought her one Salt and Honey. That's it."

"Oh. A couple shots of Jameson's should top off the night." Brogan held up his hand when Cathal started to speak.

Selena set her empty glass on the bar and stood, her eyes locked on Brogan. "Don't yell at him." In her sky-high heels, she was much taller, not as tall as him, but their faces were noticeably closer. She fisted her hands to keep them by her side and not reach for him. Just because they weren't at the restaurant didn't mean the rules had changed.

Rian had called him to give her a ride. Of all people, the one that made her light up like Christmas in July.

Brogan leaned to the side and looked at her shoes. She didn't miss the quick way his eyes skimmed over her body on his way up. She wished she could read his mind since it made his frown deepen.

"Those cannot be comfortable considering you'd rather wear flip flops."

She tilted her nose up. "They hurt like hell, but Katie said I looked nice."

"Nice?"

Rian laughed again. Selena decided she liked him, reserved but with a sense of humor when he wasn't working. She actually liked both Brogan's brothers.

"Let's go," Brogan said. "I'll drive you home."

Her heart stuttered. "I don't need you to drive me home. I'm a big girl. I can call a cab." She didn't want him to see her small apartment. It was all she could afford in Atlanta. He probably lived in a penthouse somewhere, lined with his designer suits where he made his guests take their shoes off at the door.

"Cabs aren't safe."

"I know self-defense moves." She held up her hand like she might do a karate chop.

Brogan caught her wrist, tugging her a fraction closer. God, this was torture. "Show me later. If I drive you, you don't have to pay for a cab. I'm free." He didn't release her wrist. "Cathal, watch out for Katie." He glanced Cathal's direction. "From a distance."

Cathal leaned back against the bar. "Of course, Brog."

"Rian watch out for Cathal."

Rian smirked. "Who's going to watch out for me?"

"The fact you're drinking beer means you'll be fine." With a small tug, Brogan led Selena out of the bar and into the late summer night. His entire hand encircled her wrist in a warm grip, putting her under Brogan's complete control at that one moment.

She glanced at her cell phone, trying to give herself something else to think about besides her wishful thinking that he had any other feelings for her. "I gotta get home. It's almost midnight."

He smiled over his shoulder, slipping his grip from her wrist to her hand.

She stared at their hands, linked together. His was large. Strong. Was holding hands against the company's rules? She hoped not because she didn't plan on dropping it first.

"Do you turn into a pumpkin at midnight?"

She blinked, focusing back on him. "No, but the nurse has to go home. Or almost a nurse." She squinted, trying to get the story straight. "She's Katie's sister."

"Why do you have a nurse?" He unlocked his car. She'd expected a Mercedes or BMW. No, just a really clean four-door Audi. Responsible and conservative. Just like Brogan.

He opened her car door. "You don't have to tell me."

The seat seemed so far away from this height. No way she'd make it down without falling on her butt in her shoes. She set one hand on his shoulder and kicked up a foot behind her, slipping out of the shoes from hell.

He gripped her waist, keeping her steady. His amazing hands were almost as distracting as trying to balance after four *very* heavy drinks.

"Tell you what?" She looked up at him, remembering his last statement. She was back at her normal height.

He hadn't released her waist. Again, she either imagined him drawing her closer, or she swayed his direction. Not enough for their bodies to touch, but enough for her to feel the heat radiating through his shirt. Wait.

"You're wearing a t-shirt." She stepped away, shamelessly checking him out from head to toe and back up again. And probably one or two more times. "And blue jeans." Damn. The man could wear anything and look hot. "It looks good on you."

He grinned and motioned to the car. "Get in, Cinderella."

His hand cupped her elbow, helping her down. He was sweet. And helpful. A perfect gentleman. She wished he could be more, but even drunk, she knew that was impossible. Brogan never broke the rules. If he had any idea where her thoughts had been, he'd probably fire her out of principle.

5

"How did it go at the other bank?" Brogan sat on the edge of his desk. After the first bank declined their loan yesterday, he'd sent Cathal to two more banks. Same answer from both. Securing a loan with the expectations of future profits and nothing tangible such as property, was risky.

Cathal kicked back on the long, leather sofa, a glass of whiskey in his hand. The top line at their bar. And he'd paid for it. No free drinks. They all agreed on that when they first opened, mainly to prevent Cathal from running their profits into the toilet.

"They're considering it, but this banker seemed more interested than the others. Filing our tax returns Monday helped. Showed our profits even higher this year." Cathal rested his ankle over his knee. "Rian said the banker in Ireland agreed to provide a loan against our property there. That lowers the amount we need here if it comes to that."

He never wanted to involve the land, but the more he thought about it, the more he knew his Ma would want them to keep the Pub. She'd have loved it there. "Good. That's good."

"Now, for the important question." Cathal leaned forward. "How did it go last night with Selena?"

Brogan pushed off his desk. "I've tried to forgive you and Rian for that." And forget about how good it felt to touch her because it was still hell to keep his distance at nine in the morning.

"Forgive me? You'd have had my head if we'd seen her and not called you. And after she mentioned getting a cab. Alone." He shook his head. "No. Don't turn your A-type personality around to be my fault. Or Rian's. You forget that he was the one who actually suggested you come and give her the ride home."

"You realize that nothing can happen with Selena. Yes, I appreciate you watching out for her, but don't think that it's some lead-in for me to start seeing an employee. Despite what you and Rian will allow." Not that Brogan hadn't thought of it. Constantly. But he needed to focus on keeping his business open, not how he can manage to date an employee in secret. The four lawsuits from his past still haunted him. No woman would ever have a reason to accuse him again. He already slept like shit the night before.

Selena had innocently gripped his shoulder to take her shoe off. Holding onto her waist to keep her from swaying and possibly falling was out of instinct. Then she'd looked up at him with those eyes and heart-shaped face, and he couldn't let go. And for that brief second, he'd forgotten about his rules.

Cathal huffed. "This is ridiculous."

"It's fair."

"Fair? You've given her extra work. You promoted her to a management position."

"Exactly. If I turned around and tossed her in my bed, the entire staff would talk, not to mention she could throw a big sexual harassment suit my way."

"It's not nice to brag. Who are you tossing in your bed?" Rian entered the room without knocking, closing the door behind him. "Selena? What did I miss last night?" He smiled. "Did you finally take your younger brothers' advice and make a move?"

"No. And I won't." Brogan walked around his desk, putting himself back where he was comfortable. In charge. "Nothing happened or will happen."

"Two hundred he doesn't make it to Christmas." Cathal tilted his head to the side. "Three hundred that she invites him to a home-cooked, Thanksgiving dinner."

Rian scoffed. "I'm not going to bet you." He pointed at Brogan. "That man has never gone against his word a day in his life. A pretty face and nice—smile won't change the very fiber of his being. Strict and straight. That's what Ma called him, wasn't it?"

Cathal nodded. "Yup. By the book, old Brogan is."

"Shut up and drink your whiskey." Brogan sat down at his computer. The spreadsheet Selena had made was open on his screen. She'd help with the reviews, organizing them into praises and improvements, and still sugar coating it, so she doesn't hurt his feelings.

"Fire her." Rian lifted a shoulder. "Fire Selena. Then ask her out."

"She needs the job. And she's good at it. I know you think I promoted her because of whatever reaction you saw from me—"

"Lust," Cathal said.

"Longing," added Rian.

Brogan pinched his nose. They were making it worse. Which, if he knew his brothers, was their main objective.

"Whatever. Selena is the best employee I have. Especially now that I have her coming in early. She's only been late a couple of times, but she's still on time for her shift."

"And you get to spend a little more time with your pretty waitress. Win-win." Rian took a long sip. "It won't go away, you know. The attraction. You might as well give in to it."

"You two have the luxury of giving in. I don't. I just listed out," he paused. They'd never listened to him. "Never mind. I'm done talking about it. Go away. Both of you. I'm ready to call it a day." Brogan had been there for eleven hours. He rarely drank, but tonight, after his brothers' nice, annoying reminders about Selena, he needed a beer.

"We still need to talk about—"

"No!" Brogan barked at Rian. "I'm done talking about her. You both know what happened the last time I had an employee make it seem as though she was interested. A fat lawsuit. Right now, the last thing we need is another Crissy. I can't risk it." His own feeling didn't matter in the decision. He'd never thought Selena would be like Crissy. But he never thought Crissy was going to be like Crissy.

He was young. Dumb. Inexperienced. Now he knew how vindictive one person could be. And how easily they could destroy everything he worked for.

Rian snagged Cathal's whiskey from his hand, tossing the rest of it back before setting the empty glass on the coffee table. "I was actually going to ask about the last bank Cathal went to, but obviously your mind is still stuck on Selena." He held out his hands. "We date." He motioned between him and Cathal. "We see women. We ask women out. We have a social life outside this place. You don't. It only makes sense that you'd be attracted to one of the women you employ."

"Doesn't mean I have a right to act on it."

"Just," Rian said, leaning back in his chair, "push it a little and see. If the opportunity presents itself with Selena, then move in slowly. Test the waters. We're not saying to jump in feet first like with Crissy. You're old now."

"Older."

"Semantics," Cathal added with a wink.

"*Older* then, if you must," Rian continued. "You'll be able to tell if that woman likes you or she's playing you."

It was tempting, moving in on Selena. Just a little. Enough, like Rian said, to test the waters. He wouldn't admit it aloud, but it made him nervous. He'd misjudged Crissy so bad, costing them all money, that he questioned even his own intuition on women.

"I'LL GRAB MORE NAPKINS." Selena shifted around a table and walked to the back of the restaurant. Rolling silverware wasn't the most glamorous part of the job, but it needed to be done. It gave the waitstaff a moment to relax off their feet. Talk about the weather. Gossip. Anything to help make their short break feel a little longer.

The supply room wasn't large, but it was stacked floor to the ceiling, with additional shelves lining the walls. Organized, of course. Her boss wouldn't have it any other way. Her polite boss that had kept his polite hands to himself when taking her home from the bar. And Monday morning, when she arrived for work, he was right back to square one.

Aloof. Bossy. She groaned with frustration and flipped

the switch for the fluorescent light in the supply room. It flickered, crackled, and went out.

Great. Just awesome. She pulled a box of toilet paper from the corner and propped open the door. She'd tell Brogan later about the light after she got a stack of napkins to Katie, who was on silverware rolling duty for the time being. It kept Selena from having to sit with Trey. He was nice, but he constantly wanted to talk about video games and how many points he'd scored.

She squeezed past the shelf with the condiments and to the corner. Paper towels and more toilet paper. She didn't blame whoever did the ordering. It was hell when the bathroom ran out of TP.

The light vanished, and the door shut with a solid *bam*.

Crap. Some good employee who had no clue she stood in the back corner just closed the door. Feeling with her hands, she grabbed the one box of napkins she'd spotted. Now, to make it back out.

Her shoulder bumped the tall shelves. She reached out, steadying it. The entire puzzle of boxes would crash down on her if she weren't careful, burying her under paper products and ketchup until someone noticed her missing.

She tripped over the box of toilet paper she'd pulled out and whoever closed the door had shoved back in, stumbling forward.

The door opened as she reached to brace herself on the table left of the door. Her legs stumbled over a few smaller boxes, and she ducked trying to avoid the shelf she knew lined the wall at head height.

Strong hands gripped her shoulders, keeping her from face planting into the box of squeeze packets of hot sauce she recognized the second before the door shut again, leaving them in darkness.

"Are you alright?"

Her breath lodged in her throat. Chill bumps ran over her skin from Brogan's rich voice in the dark. The heat from his body and the smell that floated around his office after he showered in the morning enveloped her.

She leaned back against him to keep from knocking her head on the overhead shelf. His stiff body held still.

"I'd rather not clean up whatever is in these boxes stacked around us." She shifted to the side, her hand touching hard muscle along his waist for balance.

He hadn't released her shoulder. His fingers tightened.

But she was stuck halfway under a shelf, her feet feeling like she was about to lose a game of Twister. "Without a light, I'm not sure how to untangle myself without the entire mountain of boxes crashing down on us."

Slowly, his hands slid down from her shoulders until they gripped her waist. "I'll pick you up," he said, pulling her closer until their bodies touched for the first time.

Neither one of them moved for a long second.

His chest rose with a deep breath like he might use it to heft her out of the corner. But he didn't do anything.

"Let me set the napkins down." She tried to toss them toward the door, but they hit another box, and it fell. Along with two more. "Sorry. I'll clean it up."

"Hold onto my shoulders, and I'll pick you up and out."

She did as he asked but misjudged in the complete darkness. Her hands landed on the top of his chest, and since she'd already established her body didn't listen to her rational mind, they slid along his body until they gripped his shoulders.

Again, he didn't move. If there had been any daylight, not an ounce of it would shine between the tight way they held onto each other. Her fingertips brushed across the back of his neck, loving the feel of his hair. In the dark, it didn't seem so wrong for him to hold her. No rules. No lines designating designer suits on one side and second-hand stores on the other.

"Ready?" His voice was soft, deep.

She was, but probably not for the same thing. She nodded and then rolled her eyes in the dark. "Yes."

He picked her up and turned, setting her down at his feet. His hands never strayed from her waist, but he didn't release her immediately. She threaded her fingers through the back of his hair. "Brogan?" His name sounded breathless from her lips.

His hands didn't shift, but his thumbs skimmed along the bottom edge of her ribcage.

She needed him to say something. Anything. What did he think of her? She'd practically latched onto him at this point.

Did he think she did this to work her way up in the company or something? She half-laughed. Only if he was an idiot.

"What's so funny?"

"Do you think I did this on purpose?"

"How would you have known I would come by and close the door?" His voice held a touch of suspicion that riled her up. He straightened and put a few inches between their bodies. The man didn't have a shred of humor in his personality, but she wouldn't let him get to her. Brogan needed something light and happy in his life.

"If you really thought that, Brogan, then you're an idiot. I was making a joke." His brothers seemed so happy. What happened to cause him to be so serious?

"I'm not sure I like my employees calling me an idiot."

She skimmed her fingers along the side of his ribs.

He jerked away, breaking their connection. "Stop that." He tried to sound mad, but the laugh in his voice told her otherwise.

"I was worried for a moment."

The door opened a second later. He reached up, adjusting the bar at the top, so it stayed open. His expression remained cautious. "Worried about what?"

"That you weren't even ticklish." She wiggled her fingers his direction. "I don't trust someone who isn't ticklish. A lack of a sense of humor I can work with." It was big words, covering up her insecurity. Had he really thought she put herself in that situation to trap him? He tried to keep himself distant, but he looked just as nervous as she felt.

Katie's face appeared in the doorway. "Did you find...whoa. What happened?"

The floor was covered in paper straws from the boxes that fell in the dark.

"I was clumsy as usual."

Katie shook her head and gave Brogan a wide berth when she came into the room. "I can help. Don't worry."

Brogan scowled.

Selena returned the look, but with a little more exaggeration. She'd get the man to smile at some point. Laugh. Have a freaking good time.

He stalked away.

"Moody much?" Katie moved into the room, beginning to pick up the straws. "Of course someone, as put together like him, would be peeved to see straws all over the ground."

Selena had the wicked thought to dump the straws all over his desk to see if that pissed him off or made him laugh. Instead, she bent down and helped clean up her mess. She'd end up dying of sexual frustration instead of old age at this pace.

6

He'd hid in his office all morning, barely speaking to Selena and giving her nothing but busy work to do after their moment in the supply room. He couldn't do anything about the obvious attraction between them but keep his distance until he learned to control it. She'd caught him watching her the few times he'd left his office during her shift, so he avoided the entire situation.

Holding her in the supply room, about killed him. When her fingers touched the back of his neck, and she said his name, he'd almost hauled her to her toes and kissed her. He'd tried to read the situation like his brother's suggested. But he couldn't. His doubts kept surfacing.

With Katie's timing, reminding him of their precarious position, he was glad he'd remembered who he was. He was her employer.

He didn't care what his brothers thought. Crissy had given him the ultimate lesson on female deception. Although he didn't think Selena was showing an interest only to lure him into a lawsuit, he couldn't risk it. He couldn't risk the restaurant. His brothers' futures.

And she thought the entire thing was a joke. The woman was a mess. He'd found her cell phone, again, sitting in the employee's break-room and caught Katie to give it to her before she left.

Brogan looked over the reservation system, the evening hostess watching him suspiciously. His constant presence probably bothered every waiter or waitress on the floor, but he didn't care. He needed to be where the action was. He needed a distraction. And since Selena didn't work the night shift, he took it out on his employees.

Being a perfectionist wasn't bad.

"Mr. O'Keeley?" Cara asked as she fell in step beside him. Shift manager for his night employees, she was easy to spot with a bright, unnatural shade of red hair and nearly six feet tall. Unlike Lenny, Cara already had excellent leadership skills. "We've had three employees go homesick. I called in a few of the staff who work in the mornings." She flipped the paper on her clipboard. "Katie, Selena, and Trey. Trey just arrived. Katie said something about having to help Selena, but then they'd both be here."

"Boss," one of the kitchen workers began, tapping him on the shoulder. "We just had two cooks get sick."

A health epidemic on the night that Randy Simmons was due to arrive for another meal pushed Brogan's patience. And now he'd have his eyes on Selena to top it off.

"Obviously, let's keep this low key. As you see employees, quietly tell them that the minute they start to feel ill, to let you know and leave the floor. I'll call Rian to help in the kitchen."

The young kid's eyes grew round. "Seriously?"

"Am I ever not serious?"

"No, sir."

"Then go back and handle it the best you can until he gets here."

The kid turned around, as if in a daze, and walked back to the kitchen. Rian might be considered the quiet one, but he didn't have that reputation in the kitchen. The awards he'd won over the years preceded him. As well as his demand for excellence.

Brogan pulled out his phone and dialed his brother's number. He answered after one ring. "Rian, we need you at the restaurant. Two of your kitchen staff have left sick. I have three sick on the floor. I'd hate to lose more and not have the manpower for Saturday night."

"On my way. I'll pull Cathal."

"Why?"

"He can work the bar if nothing else. See you in ten." Rian hung up.

Selena breezed through the door, Katie right behind her. Both with serious, game-faces on as they scanned the dining room. It instantly reminded him of another significant reason he couldn't cross the line. The business was better because of Selena.

"Good," Cara said. "They're here earlier than I thought. The Simmons party just arrived, too."

Brogan hadn't noticed, his eyes locked on Selena's pursed lips as she walked his direction. "Is the upstairs room ready?" he asked.

"Yes."

Selena and Katie came to a stop in front of him. "Where do you want us," Katie asked, looking between Brogan and Cara.

"The Simmons party is back again."

Selena winced and looked away.

"What is it?" Brogan had seen the tip reported from that

night. With the apartment complex she lived in, surely, she needed the money.

Katie, Cara, and Brogan all waited for Selena to answer. She shot an annoyed look in his direction. "Nothing."

"Something," he answered. Katie and Cara looked at him. He didn't need this, to let anyone know that he had a little more than just a professional interest in Selena. But he couldn't ignore her discomfort.

She stared at the party as they passed by the group. Mr. Simmons was so involved in a conversation, he didn't notice Brogan. But two of the men, separately, both sent Selena a look he didn't appreciate.

A look that if Selena were his, he'd point it out to them both. Immediately.

"Oh." He kept the fury out of his tone of voice and slipped his hands into his pockets to conceal the fists.

Selena shook her head. "I can deal with it."

"There's no reason for you to deal with it, though." He looked at Katie. "If any of those men are inappropriate, let me know. Immediately."

She nodded her head. "Yes, sir."

"Do you want to work it with Katie? If not, Cara can pull someone else."

Selena took a deep breath. "I'm fine. Really. I'll give those two fine specimens to Katie."

Katie grinned. "I'll handle them."

"I'm sure you will." Brogan patted Katie on the shoulder. "Let me know if you need any additional help."

She smiled. "Thanks, Mr. O'Keeley."

Cara walked back up to the front, and Katie headed to the employee break room.

"I mean it about those men. I'll ask them to leave if they say or do anything inappropriate." He realized belatedly how deep his accent had grown. She didn't miss it based on the way her lips pursed together.

"Between Katie and me, we'll be fine. Don't worry about it."

Rian came in the front door, already wearing his chef's shirt and ugly, required shoes. "I'm here to report to duty."

Brogan smirked. "Do you wear that outfit underneath your regular clothes, hoping for some type of culinary emergency?"

Selena giggled, covering her mouth with her hand. "Sorry." Her light eyes held a smile. "But that was funny."

"The short answer is yes, I do." He grinned. "Are you here to help with the epidemic?"

Selena nodded, looking a little more relaxed than before.

Brogan straightened his shoulders. He'd done that. Made her laugh. Helped her relax from the tense woman a few moments ago.

"Absolutely," she said. "And they just seated my table. I need to get going."

She locked eyes with Brogan a quick second before her shoulder brushed his as she passed by him. Out of instinct, he grasped her wrist lightly in his hand and kept their hands low and concealed. She stopped, her head snapping up.

"Cathal will be behind the bar. If you need help with those men and can't find me, tell him." He skimmed his thumb along her inner wrist, enjoying the way her mouth parted with her exhale. "He'd probably enjoy tossing a pompous ass or two out of the restaurant."

She nodded her head once, and he dropped her wrist, immediately missing the contact of their skin.

Rian's eyebrows were close to his hairline.

"Don't even start."

"I don't even know where to start." He patted Brogan on the back. "But I know this has to be tearing you up, so you have my sympathy. Glad you took our advice."

"It was horrible advice that ended in an awkward situation that I didn't know how to handle."

"I'd say you handled it fairly well judging by the way that pretty woman just looked at you."

"She doesn't think I have a sense of humor."

Rian contorted his face into an exaggerated frown. "I can't imagine why that is."

"Shut up and get to work." He didn't even know what got into him when it came to Selena. His brothers, putting all sorts of ideas into his head, hadn't helped. He could compartmentalize her. She belonged in a neat box marked with an X. He needed to remember both their places.

He was the boss.

She was the employee.

Everything else in his life functioned like clockwork except for Selena. With one last glance up at Simmons' party, he walked to the front of the business, again, looking for something to do that kept his mind off the pretty waitress he could never be with.

"FIVE OF THE guys slipped me their telephone numbers." Katie snarled. "Dirty old men. Most of them are old enough to be my dad. And I told two of them that exact thing, but they just smiled and told me I could call them daddy."

"Do you think they just hit on anything moving hoping something will bite?" Selena threw away two pieces of paper with telephone numbers. The same two men as before passed them to her as she'd set down their appetizers.

Katie giggled. "So now we're fish trying to dodge the hook."

"A hook with crappy bait." Selena made her friend laugh, and she tried to feel just as lighthearted. But she couldn't. God, Brogan confused the hell out of her. Touching her one second and pushing her away the next. Acting as if he cared. Trying to make a damn joke of all things.

All she'd done is tell herself he wouldn't cross that line because of his own rules. But what if it was more? What if it was because of her social standing? She'd faced that once before. Her ex-boyfriend, Jacob, had claimed to love her and then hidden her away when he realized she could never become the social queen he wanted. Was Brogan the same? Had she read all the signals right, but he kept remembering that she wasn't in the same league as he was?

"Excuse me," a deep voice called from the table.

Katie rolled her eyes. "Ugh."

"I'll take it. You take the water pitcher around and do a refill. Try not to dump it over someone's head."

"I'll try to control myself."

Selena headed back, scanning the table, noting that they were partway through their entrees. A few drinks needed a refill. She stopped beside Randy Simmons, who sat at the head of the table. An attractive man, well into his sixties that still worked out based on the way he filled out the dress shirt he wore. A pretty boy is what Katie had called him. Boy was a little stretch. He looked more like a grandpa Malibu Ken doll than a real man. Fake tan, bright white teeth, and a Rolex watch that must have cost him a small fortune. She hated flashy men like that.

He probably drove an overpriced sports car, too.

"Yes, sir?"

He shook his head slowly. "I've asked you to call me Randy, Selena."

He had.

And she hadn't.

"Did you need something?" She looked at his plate, mostly empty. His drink was empty. "A vodka and tonic?"

"Yes, and," he said, lowering his voice, making it hard to hear above the conversation at the table, "I'd like to take you out sometime."

Damn. Even their leader was scuzzy. "I'm sorry, but I'm only available to provide you with another drink." With most men, that provided them an easy way out of an awkward situation.

"Are you sure about that?"

She arched an eyebrow and stood straight. "Same type of vodka?"

"Do you know who I am?" He sat back in his chair like he'd tell her a story—definitely Malibu Ken Grandpa. "I'm about to renovate this entire corner of Atlanta. Put in a big plaza shopping center."

"Oh." Her face felt hot. Straight anger from the cocky way he didn't care about the people he'd put out of a job. But it wasn't her place to butt in. "So you don't want the drink?"

He smiled brighter. "I like your spunk. Once we close O'Keeley's down, I'll have use for someone like you on my staff. If you're interested."

She crossed her arms. "And what does your staff do, exactly?"

"Whatever I need them to do." His hand encircled the outside of her thigh and squeezed.

She smacked his arm away and stepped to the side. Her face flamed hotter. Adrenaline. "I'll get your check."

His lips quirked to the side. "I'm not through with my meal." He motioned to the table. "Neither are my colleagues, and they'll leave when I do. You wouldn't want them to have to leave without paying since you didn't allow them time to finish? I'm sure your boss wouldn't like that."

The restaurant didn't need the loss of revenue on a party this size. It didn't mean they had to finish their dinner at O'Keeley's. Even Brogan had mentioned tossing them out. He'd have her back. She lifted her chin. "I'll be sure to bring you all a to-go box." She turned and stormed out of the room and down the stairs.

As promised, Cathal stood behind the bar, looking like he entertained the crowd better than serving drinks efficiently. But it was manpower on a night they desperately needed it. She took a strong, deep breath to cool her temper as she crossed the floor.

She didn't want to bitch and moan about Simmons to Cathal. She'd handled it. Now, the group needed to pay and leave before Brogan came out to check on things. He had enough to worry about with the bank without her adding to it.

Cathal met her at the end of the bar. He cleaned off two empty pint glasses and began to wipe down the wood. His red collared shirt with the O'Keeley's logo and blue jeans looked far more casual than he normally dressed.

"Now, what has displeased you?"

"Nothing. Why?" She tried to give him a perky smile. Judging by his look, he didn't buy it.

He leaned his elbows on the bar. "Brogan mentioned a few of the guys in the party might give you a hard time."

Selena shrugged. "I can handle it." She wished she could have tossed Simmons out on his ass and covered their tab herself. But this was a more professional way to treat him. Even if he didn't deserve it.

Katie stepped up beside her. "I figured you could use an extra set of hands with that many to-go boxes. I'm glad you kicked them out. No tip is worth letting Simmons paw all over you." She brightened when her eyes landed on Cathal. "Well, hey there." She nudged Selena's shoulder, completely oblivious that her confession about Simmons just darkened Cathal's gaze significantly.

"Hello, Katie," he replied with a sharp glance at Selena.

Katie smiled wider. "I can proudly say I had the cutest guy in the bar take me home last week. Too bad, he dropped me off and told me to drink some water and take two aspirins."

"What exactly happened up there, Selena?" he asked.

She hoped to simplify it. "I told Simmons he needed to leave. We're getting them to-go boxes and their checks."

He shifted, giving Katie his full attention. "Katie, sweetheart, what did you mean by Simmons pawing all over Selena?"

Selena looked up at the exposed wooden beams in the ceiling. No way Katie might, for once, keep quiet. She closed her eyes. Yup. There she went, giving Cathal a play-by-play. Even down to Simmons's suggestive proposition.

"He touched you?"

Cathal's direct question unnerved her. Not for getting Randy Simmons in trouble. No. If she had to guess, this wasn't Randy's first time propositioning a woman. But the aggression in Cathal's voice. Tense. Dangerous.

Selena rolled her eyes, hoping to come across as nonchalant. "He touched my blue jeans—"

"Ladies, I'd appreciate it if you'd give me a few minutes with our guests before returning with their to-go boxes."

Cathal stepped from behind the bar. He paused beside Selena and mumbled, "find Brogan. But, for God's sake, don't tell him about Simmons touching you."

"I tried not to tell *you* about Simmons touching me."

"Just send him up that way."

Selena dropped her head forward. "Will do." Oh well for trying to keep the peace.

Katie leaned her back against the bar and watched Cathal leave. "I really wish I knew him before I started working here. One night. That's all I want."

God, sometimes, Katie was oblivious. "I'm going to go tell the boss and grab those to-go boxes. You can offer to take drinks from the bar to tables down here on the floor. Save everyone a few trips."

She gave her a mock salute. "I'm on it."

Selena walked to the door of Brogan's office. He sat at his computer, his brow wrinkled as he looked at his computer screen. He'd messed up his hair on one side. His tie sat a little crooked. She really didn't want to add on the stress.

"Hey," she started.

He stood up so quickly his computer chair almost flipped. "Is everything alright?"

She held up her hands to calm him down. "Yes. Cathal went upstairs to the party. Asked me to find you and tell you to meet him up there."

He stepped from around the desk. She didn't budge from blocking his way. "You forgot your jacket."

He blinked before stepping back to his chair and putting it on. "Thank you. What happened?"

"Cathal said for you to go on up. I have about forty to-go boxes to collect."

The concerned look shifted to something intense. He set a hand on her shoulder, squeezing it. "You're alright?"

No. Not when he watched her with so much concern. "I'm fine." She straightened his tie, avoiding his gaze, smoothing the tie down his body, feeding off his strength.

"I don't believe you."

She tilted her head back, soaking in the way he watched her. She brushed down the small part of his soft hair that stuck out on the side, not caring at the moment what was appropriate.

"Then that's too bad." Selena gave him a light shove out the door, trying to play it off like it wasn't a big deal. "Go. Before Cathal gets distracted and finds a pretty girl to talk to."

She watched him take the stairs two at a time until he reached the top, pausing a long moment. He glanced over his shoulder, finding her immediately, a dark scowl in place.

Even from that distance, she felt the electricity between them snap. Rian stepped up beside her. "Cathal sent me a text to come to help out with Brogan. Any idea what's going on?"

"Help with Brogan?" There went her ability to handle the situation alone. "They're up there. With Simmons."

"Oh." With that one word, Rian left and also took the stairs two at a time. Only he didn't pause at the top but rushed forward and out of sight.

What a damn night.

Selena grabbed the to-go boxes and went back to the bar to shuttle drinks out to help the overworked waitstaff. She'd rather do that all night than deal with Simmons again.

All three men appeared at once, walking down the stairs. After a brief word to each other, Brogan disappeared into his office, slamming the door.

"Dang. They mean business, don't they," Katie said, propping her elbow up on the bar.

"I feel bad. Maybe I made it too big a deal and overreacted." What if Brogan was actually mad she cut their meal short?

Katie patted her back. "No. It was a big deal. Men like Simmons think they get to touch any woman they want."

"Would you have kicked them out?"

"No. But I don't have that authority."

Selena winced. "I don't guess I do, either."

Katie chuckled. "Yeah, right."

Lingering on Katie's statement took too much focus at the moment. She waited until Cathal was back behind the bar, Rian pausing beside her. "So—?"

Rian smirked. "We printed out their tickets. Cathal will go up in a few minutes to run their payments."

They'd supported her decision. A little of the anxiety that she'd messed up left her body.

"Let's say that asking them to go ahead and settle up and leave was the nicest thing we could've done. Simmons did it to himself. He made a mistake and mentioned you to Brogan."

"Me? What for?"

Cathal poured a beer. She wasn't sure who it was for. "After Simmons told us that he would miss the food, but with the money he'd make, he'd be able to fly to Ireland and eat anytime he wanted to, the idiot actually told Brogan about his proposition." Cathal grinned. "And that you'd seemed interested."

Selena knew her mouth fell open, but she couldn't help it. She'd kicked them out. How did that convey interest?

Rian leaned on the bar beside her, his eyes looking green. "Don't worry, none of us think you are."

"Hell no! Slimy old bastard."

Cathal glanced in the direction of Brogan's office. "I'm

not sure how much of Brogan's tirade Simmons actually understood. Rian and I thoroughly enjoyed the creativity." He chuckled. "Only certain things will push Brogan outside his nice neat world." He didn't continue the thought, but Selena knew what it meant.

She'd pushed him.

"What's so funny?" Katie asked as she set an empty bottle on the bar beside Selena. "I'm ready to lug up the forty to-go boxes if you are."

"No. Brogan told them to pay or else. They'll pay seeing how they'd all eaten at least half of the food. We're not wasting to-go boxes on them." Rian held his hands up. "Brogan's words. Not mine."

"Or else what?" Selena asked. "A lawsuit over a seventeen-dollar fish and chips plate?"

Cathal gave her an amused look. "Or else they'll have to deal with him. My oldest brother annoys the hell out of me half the time, but the other half, I'll claim him. I'll head up to process their payments in another minute or so."

Rian pushed away from the bar. "I'm headed back to the kitchen. Call me again if I can help."

Katie set the boxes she'd picked up back down on the counter. "I knew I loved working here. Why don't you let us come back up and help clear the checks? There are forty people, all paying separately. That way we can work the three computers up there and get them out quicker."

Cathal looked to Brogan's closed door. "Sure. I suppose."

Katie patted her hands on the bar like a drum roll. "Then let's go so we can help all the other deserving customers."

He motioned Selena forward, lowering his voice. "He's not going to like you being back up there."

"I doubt Simmons will say anything else."

Or, maybe Simmons didn't give a shit about Brogan's tirade. Even with Cathal's presence, Simmons stared at her the entire time. Facing the computer, she could almost feel his eyes on her back—and butt. Soon, he'd be gone to harass some other female.

"Last one," Katie said, as she slid the credit card through the reader.

Selena turned around, only to be face-to-face with Simmons. He'd risen at some point to come to stand beside her. "I can tell your bosses don't want to lose such a valuable employee." He ran a finger down her shoulder.

She jerked away but had nowhere to go in the small booth that housed the computer. Her breath quickened.

She deepened her voice and straightened her shoulders. She didn't need Cathal to come to her rescue again. "Go. Away."

He took a small step back. "The offer stands, Selena. You'll be out of a job when I close this place down, and I have one with plenty of benefits, waiting for you." His tongue darted out, wetting his lips that looked cosmetically enhanced. His eyes tracked down her body, making her want to turn away. "Most women would jump at the opportunity to have their turn with me."

She slapped him.

Again, at some point in her life, her brain and body would sync together, but she couldn't stand it any longer. Hot pain seared across her palm from the hit.

The slap had silenced the entire room.

Simmons rubbed his cheek, but smiled, his voice no longer quiet. "You like things rough, I see."

She shifted her body weight, ready to knee him in the crotch if necessary, but Cathal jerked him back. Pure aggression covered the Irishman's face. He shouted words she didn't understand, shoving him across the room until Simmons tripped and fell.

A few of the other men around the table rose but didn't move to intervene. She didn't really blame them. Cathal looked a little possessed, getting in Simmons's face as he continued to shout.

Katie gripped Selena's arm. "Oh, hell, I think I'm in love with him."

She couldn't worry about Katie's infatuation with Cathal at the moment. Not when Brogan came barging into the chaos. People stumbled left and right as he pushed them out of the way like they weighed nothing.

Cathal hadn't hit Simmons, which surprised Selena, but his shouts had become more English and were quite unique in their use of curse words.

Brogan clamped a hand on Cathal's shoulder, tugging him away. He crossed his arms and stared down at Simmons. Instead of the shouting, his deep voice, too low to hear, put a look of surprise on Simmons's face and complete, deranged pleasure on Cathal's.

Selena started to march over there and tell Simmons off as well. If Cathal got to use his potty words, she could, too.

Brogan must have seen her movement because he looked up and held up his hand. She stopped dead in her tracks.

Fury blazed in Brogan's eyes.

With the adrenaline rush, her insides felt shaky. She stood there, unmoving, while Katie finished collecting the rest of the signed credit card receipts, and Brogan and Cathal watched the dinner party leave down the stairs and out of the restaurant.

"Katie, are you alright?" Brogan turned to face Selena.

He controlled his voice so tightly; it was barely above a whisper.

"I'm fine. Do you want me to go help behind the bar since Cathal is up here?" She gave Selena a look of pity and rubbed her hand down Selena's arm. "Or I can stay to clean up."

"The bar would be helpful." Brogan kept his eyes pinned on Selena as Katie left.

The last thing she wanted was to cause him more problems. Although, technically, she knew it wasn't her fault.

Katie paused by Cathal, who leaned against the wall, looking relaxed, as if nothing had happened. "The no dating policy applies to you too?"

He gave her a sexy smile. "I'm afraid so."

"Damn," Katie muttered before moving out of the room.

Brogan waited for Katie to disappear down the stairs, his cold, blue eyes never wavering from hers. "I don't think Simmons will be returning. You *never* have to put up with that for this job."

Selena nodded, stunned by his protective streak over her. "I'd hoped you'd be okay with me kicking them out earlier."

"Of course he is," said Rian as he stepped into the area, pausing beside Cathal. "Katie just gave me a quick rundown. I thought we were trying to get away from the fighting."

"She hit him. Our Selena there slapped the old bastard." Cathal winked at her. "A fighter."

"She'll fit in with this family," Rian said and then turned toward Cathal. "I'm surprised you left him in one piece."

"It was close." Cathal's quiet, serious response surprised her.

Brogan walked to Selena and held out his hand. "Let me see your hand."

She handed it to him. Her palm was blood red from the hit. It stung when he ran a finger across it. She hissed from the burn.

"I'm glad you hit him." His eyes flicked up.

"I'm glad you didn't," she whispered. "It's not worth going to jail over."

Cathal cleared his throat. "Do you plan on telling her what you threatened to do to him if he so much as speaks to her again?"

Rian crossed his arms. "I'd like to hear that."

The way Brogan held her hand, touched her bruised skin, eliminated any doubt that he was attracted to her.

And neither one of them could make a move.

Stalemate.

"What did you tell him?" She had to keep talking. Keep her mind from torturing her with mental images of her and Brogan together.

Cathal didn't wait for Brogan to speak. "He told him that if he ever touched you again, he'd end up in a pine box, um, with his man parts in an unnatural location. The language was a little more colorful than that."

"Creative," she whispered, lacking any other response. She'd stand there as long as Brogan watched her with desire hidden behind his concern because it was there. It pushed reality away for a brief moment, leaving the two of them alone. She stepped closer. "Thank you."

He gently held her hand as his other hand hesitantly touched her waist. He skimmed his fingers from her waist, down the outside of her hip. A trail of heat followed in its wake. His gaze dropped to her lips before flicking back up.

Instead of kissing her, like she wanted, expected, he

dropped her hand and stepped back. "You can head home if you need to. I know it was a pretty big ordeal."

"No." She crossed her arms, feeling cold from his sudden departure. Had she imagined it again? "I'm fine. Really. I'll start clearing the tables. Thank you." She smiled at Rian and Cathal, who'd just witnessed whatever happened between them. "You, too. I think you have a new member of your fan club with Katie."

Cathal shrugged, his body so casual and easygoing, it was hard to imagine him so close to being out of control a few minutes earlier. "She's sweet, but not someone worth breaking the rules for." He winked. "I'll see you later." Both he and Rian turned and walked down the stairs.

Not someone worth breaking the rules for.

Was she that person for Brogan?

She almost asked him just that. End all the back-and-forth between them. But she didn't get a chance to.

"I'll send Trey and a busboy up here to help clear," he said, a deep, angry growl still in his voice but he didn't meet her eyes.

"Alright. I'll see you in the morning."

Brogan didn't turn around again. He walked away as if she didn't exist. How could he flip it on and off? She winced at the dull pain in her hand. She'd finish her shift and go home, try to wrap her head around the confusing tangle that existed inside when it came to Brogan. And if there was anything she could do about it.

7

"Here's the new laptop." Brogan held it out for Selena to take. It was the best one in the store, according to Cathal. "Now we can both work and not take turns on my computer."

Because that was what he needed to focus on with Selena. Work. He'd revealed too much emotion with how he'd reacted to Simmons last week. And the moment in the supply room still ran through his head whenever he stepped foot in there.

He was no closer to figuring out how to handle her. Or himself. Each day, he showed up at work determined to keep his distance.

He found himself questioning not only his sanity but Selena's intentions. Something about that made him feel guilty, projecting Crissy's scheme onto her. Deep down in his gut, he knew that wasn't Selena.

"There were a couple more websites I wanted to go through and see the reviews." Selena wore her hair down and pink lip gloss that made him want to focus all his attention on her lips. "I logged onto the websites as the business." She grimaced. "I hope that's alright. There were a few reviews I responded to. They were very nice."

She was good at this job. Even though he needed her running his waitstaff, another job she excelled at, he really appreciated her help in the morning. If they could do more advertising, maybe they could increase their profit. It wouldn't be in time for the banks to loan them the money, but he'd never give up. He'd decided if they lost this location, they'd move, reopen somewhere else. But the lag time between closing and reopening might hurt the business they had now. They had a loyal customer base that he'd hoped would follow them. But, based on a preliminary review of the other locations nearby, they couldn't afford the rent.

"Did you go to college, Selena?"

She hesitated. "No. Is that a problem?" She kept her eyes averted, booting up the laptop, and almost hiding behind it.

He pushed the top of the computer down a little, forcing her to look at him. "Not in the least. You're good at this side of the business, advertising and promotion, and I didn't know if you had any training for it."

Getting to know her, even a little more, was necessary. They only had a friendship to develop. He'd like someone like Selena as a friend since he couldn't bring himself to have something more.

"Thank you," she mumbled. "I thought about going to school, actually started once, but it never worked out. I fell into waitressing. It doesn't pay a whole lot, but I enjoy it. Ugh, Brogan, the computer wants me to set up a passcode and everything."

"Then set it up."

"But it's the company's laptop." She sat back. "Did you buy this just for me?"

"I bought it for the company. I just never had a reason to have more than one computer here before you." He smiled, hoping to put her at ease. She'd been jumpy and distant since the Simmons incident. "You can keep it in the office if it makes you feel better."

"Yes. Definitely." She started typing, and for the next hour, they worked across his desk from each other in silence, a natural rhythm that lasted until she needed to get ready for her shift.

"Same time tomorrow?" She pulled her hair back, arranging it into a ponytail while he sat and watched. He'd noticed the slender curve of her neck before, the smooth skin that would smell sweet. Was she sensitive there?

He cleared his throat. "Yes." He needed to finish dressing despite the heat running in his veins from being near her. He began to button his cuffs.

Instead of leaving, she waited, as if she waited for him to finish, and they could both start their day together. The thought made him smile. They had their own morning routine.

"Any big plans this weekend? Going back out with Katie?"

She laughed, her honey-colored eyes sparkling. "No. Katie hasn't mentioned it."

"I figured it was a regular thing you both did."

"Not at all. Katie only goes out when she's not in a relationship. She just broke up with someone a few weeks ago. So, she's kicking the dust off, so to speak."

"And you?" He swallowed, afraid to get personal. "Are you, um, seeing anyone?" He picked up his tie, concentrating on sliding it behind his neck while he waited for her response.

"No. Are you?"

He tied his tie, stalling for some type of rational thought to make him pull back from the direction of their conversation. But he didn't want to. He wanted her to know there wasn't anyone else, either.

"No. I'm not," he said, slipping into his suit jacket that suddenly felt tighter than before. He shouldn't have these thoughts about her. Shouldn't risk it.

She took a step, her expression wary a split second before she tilted her chin and closed the distance between them.

Brogan stiffened. If she kissed him, here, in his office, he'd surely die from the shock of the experience.

But she didn't kiss him. She reached up and straightened his tie. "Sorry. I didn't want you to leave with it crooked."

"Thanks," he said. She smelled like wildflowers. He'd noticed before when he'd held her close. "We should probably get to work."

She patted his tie twice before she pressed her hand against his chest, sliding down a little. He held his breath at her touch.

"Thank you, again, for what you did with Simmons." Her open expression and upturned face tempted him. The rush of breath over her lips, a soft sigh, was the only sound he heard. After a long pause, she dropped her hand to her side. "Have a good day, Brogan."

He swallowed, finally finding his voice. "You, too." Why did he feel the need to torture himself this way?

SELENA SLID the bag of groceries onto the kitchen table, smiling at Katie as she brought in another load. "You didn't have to help me, but thanks."

Katie shrugged. "I have nothing else to do. I went on a second date with that Army hat guy I met the other night at the bar. I really must have had some beer-goggles on. Definitely cuter with a hat." She began to unload the bags.

Mimi shuffled into the kitchen. "Hello, Katie," she said. Selena never picked up as deep of an accent as her grandmother held. Growing up in the middle of downtown Atlanta failed to produce that deep drawl known in other parts of the state.

"Hello, Ms. Estella." Katie held up a rented DVD and a pint of ice cream. "Are you up for girl's night?"

"What movie is that?" she asked.

"The newest James Bond."

Mimi laughed, a rich deep sound that Selena remembered from when she was little. Her mom and Mimi would sit around the kitchen table, smoking cigarettes and laughing about something. Even though her mom had problems with men and was a pretty lousy role model, Selena never remembered being unhappy. That didn't come until she recognized how the world worked. And she realized that which side of the tracks you were raised does matter to some people.

Growing up in a trailer held a certain stigma.

Selena looked around her cramped, old apartment. She kept it clean, if not neat and put away. It was the best she could do at the moment.

"My favorite James is Sean Connery."

"James? Are you on a first-name basis?" Katie asked with a laugh.

Mimi winked. "Absolutely, honey."

Selena finished putting away the groceries before joining them in the living room. Three bowls of ice cream and the newest James Bond film with two women she loved.

It made the ache deep down for Brogan less prominent because it was always there, a half-second from entering into her mind and distracting her, making her wonder how to push him past his rules.

He'd asked her if she was seeing anyone. That wasn't a green flag that he was straight-out interested in her. She knew better than to infer that. But the way he'd said it, with a nervous hitch in his voice, made her wonder. He never got personal with his employees. Asking her if she had a boyfriend was a *very* personal question.

"Ms. Estella, did Selena tell you how her boss came to her rescue the other night?" Katie ignored Selena's head shake. She didn't want to upset her grandmother with a bad story.

"It was nothing."

"No," Mimi said, also ignoring Selena. "What happened?"

"There was this horrible customer that said something to Selena, and our boss kicked him out. Personally, I think he has a thing for Selena."

Mimi's eyebrows pulled down tight, making her normally lightly wrinkled face contort. "Her boss? Isn't he the one you both complained about was too demanding and a dictator?"

"The same one." Katie took a big bite of ice cream, blowing Selena an air kiss. "Apparently, he's not quite so bossy to Selena as to the rest of us."

"Oh, he's just as bossy. Believe me." Bossy in that he gets to dictate the speed of their flirty "non" relationship that's currently driving her crazy.

Mimi watched Selena for a moment. "You can always find another job, honey."

"No. I like this job. He's fine."

Katie laughed again. "You know he's a football field distance beyond *fine*. More like a total hottie. But I'm beyond drooling for him."

"Yeah. You're just drooling over Cathal."

Mimi held up her hand. "Who's Cathal?"

"Brogan's youngest brother. He owns the pub as well," Selena said.

"I love how you say his name." Katie clasped her hands together. "*Brogan*. Oh, my hot boss, *Brogan!*"

Selena tried to be mad at Katie, but she couldn't. For the past six months, she'd been her best friend. She'd helped Katie through two major break-ups, and Katie helped Selena stay sane. And Mimi loved Katie. Loved how open and funny she was about life. Nothing could shock her grandmother.

Mimi scrapped the bottom of her ice cream bowl and set it on the small table beside her. "Selena, you should tell him how you feel."

"Yeah. I don't think so. That's not happening. We have a strict no dating policy, Mimi. And he enforces that rule each time he gets the chance." That's what confused her about his actions. She could almost see the struggle inside him. He was interested. She'd established that. The way he watched her, touched her, talked to her. But still, he could control himself enough to hold back. Keep his distance.

Keep his damn rules in place.

She'd chased after Jacob all those years ago. And that was a turning point in her life. She'd never chase after a man again. Beg him to accept her. Hope he thought she was good enough with her trailer park background and no college degree.

She couldn't chase after Brogan. If that meant she'd never know what it was like to be held by those arms, then that was the price she'd pay. Her ego was too fragile to risk anything else.

"I think I'll just stay on the sideline for right now. I need this job."

Katie stuck her tongue out. "You're no fun."

"I don't see you chasing after Cathal."

"Because Cathal doesn't like me like that. He doesn't look at me like he wants to devour me the way Ms. Estella just killed that ice cream."

Mimi laughed. "Mint chocolate chip is my favorite."

"I know," Katie and Selena said at the same time. Katie left the topic alone for the evening and soon, soft snores came from Mimi's end of the sofa. She'd miss this. If she ever could get her grandmother into the proper facility, she'd miss her being beside her in the evenings. There when she awoke in the mornings. But it was for the best.

Last month, she'd fallen in the middle of the night. Selena couldn't sleep for a week, expecting to wake up and find her grandmother on the ground and instead of a small cut on her arm, maybe a gash on her forehead. Or a broken bone. Selena was strong, but not strong enough to handle Mimi in every situation possible.

She'd try again with the insurance company. God knows she didn't have enough money to pay for a nursing facility herself.

SELENA RUSHED through the door of O'Keeley's. She was later than usual but had a good reason. The insurance company had called, scheduling another appointment to meet and discuss Mimi's qualifications into the facility she needed. Brogan stepped out of his bathroom as she walked into his office. His undershirt was tucked into his suit pants, but his dress shirt hung open.

His hair was wet and unstyled.

His feet, bare.

Hell.

She came to a dead stop in the middle of the room to get her reaction under control.

He looked delicious.

"Good morning," he said, his eyes brightening. She did that to him, made him happy.

"Hi."

"You seem happy." His crooked smile appeared. He spoke a little less structured around her, his accent deeper. Did he realize it?

"It is a good morning." Mimi had been the happiest. When she was all present, she always lamented living with Selena. Young people should be around other young people, she would say. But Selena had Katie, and now she wanted Brogan.

At breakfast, Mimi had brought up their conversation with Katie from a few days before. She'd pushed Selena to talk to Brogan about her feelings. She couldn't do that. But she might nudge him along. Not enough to get fired on the spot, but if he didn't make a move, it was because he didn't like her in return and not because he wasn't sure of her feelings.

He sat down at his computer. "I came up with an idea this morning. I'm not sure if you can do it. So, please, just tell me if you can't."

"I probably can." She'd done everything else he'd asked. His confidence in her, passing off assignment after assignment, gave her a sense of pride.

He clicked through a few screens, pulling up various

websites in different windows. "I don't even know if we can do it without hiring someone. Or I can do it."

He exasperated her with his controlling nature. "Stop procrastinating and tell me what you want. I know I can do it." Selena stood behind Brogan, her hand resting loosely on the back of his chair. Two weeks after being asked to come in early, she had moved into almost an administrative assistant role. Simply working beside Brogan satisfied a small side of her. She'd figured out some of the little things that made him tick. That made him mad. The way he liked his coffee. The way he tied his tie. All the things someone in a relationship would know about their partner.

Too bad their relationship was more G rated than some Disney movies.

Brogan pointed at the screen. She leaned a little closer. At nine thirty, no one else would arrive for another thirty minutes. They had this short time together each morning— their own little world where he let down his wall for a few minutes.

"Here. I'm trying to push our advertising to these sites. I have the ad packages; I'm not sure how to contact them." He leaned back. His hair brushed her hand. She should move and not be so obsessed, but she stayed. One small, minute shift of her hand and her fingers would brush through the soft, damp hair.

"I could figure it out," he continued, lifting one shoulder, "but I'd appreciate the help."

Help. The boss wanted help. Not fondled by his employee. He looked up at her. If they were together, an item, she'd lean down and kiss him. Would he flip out if she did that, now? His blue eyes watched her a long second before he looked away.

"I'll find out for you." She hoped her voice sounded light.

"Thanks," he murmured.

"Oh, I meant to tell you I have a meeting tomorrow morning. Do I need to find someone to be the shift manager?"

He turned the chair around to face her. "I hope everything is alright."

"It is." She'd not told him about Mimi. She didn't want to ruin whatever image he held of her with the knowledge that every morning and night she took care of an elderly woman with memory loss. It wasn't the sexist thought in the world.

He wanted to ask; she could tell. She bit back a laugh. He always followed every rule about the separation of work and personal life. Except asking if she had a boyfriend— he'd broken his rule for that.

"Do you want to know what my meeting is for?"

"That's your business." He turned back to his computer, grumpy again. Poor guy.

She twisted to lean against his desk, partway blocking his view of his computer. She'd take the face-on view when she admitted to him that she took care of her grandmother.

"I have to meet with the insurance company."

"Oh? Why's that?" He tried to look around her at the screen, but she shifted, her knee pressing against his leg.

This was the point that people usually backed away from her. But Brogan wasn't *in,* to begin with. "I live with someone."

His jaw tightened. He leaned back in his office chair, and he linked his hands behind the back of his head. His white dress shirt flared open, confirming all the hours he spent in the gym were worth it. "I didn't realize that. I thought you said you weren't seeing anyone."

She blinked at his sudden irritation. "Oh." She smiled and patted his knee. "Not a man."

His shoulders relaxed. "Then who lives with you?"

"My grandmother."

"Your—" He sat forward, bringing them closer than usual. Her breathe caught, but she didn't move. "Your granny lives with you?"

"Yes." Was it that bad? Would he turn away like the few other men she'd tried to date? She cleared her throat. Not that she had any plans, or ability, to date Brogan, but it would hurt if he did.

He rose. Good God, so much man stood *right* in front of her. She itched to touch him, wrap her arms around his body. Her day was good because of the insurance meeting. It'd just kicked up another notch. The spicy scent of his aftershave made her want to lean closer.

"Is that why you were late all those times?"

"Yes." Her voice sounded breathless. It was his fault. "I had to wait for the nurse to get there."

"You should have told me, Selena."

If she wasn't already propped up on the desk, her knees might have given way. He even cared about that. "I don't like excuses." She tilted her head to the side, studying his expression. "You wouldn't have had to invite me here early every morning if I had."

His thighs touched hers, the only evidence that he'd shifted a fraction closer. "Where are your parents?"

Brogan asking another personal question was major movement forward in their not-quite relationship. "I have no idea about my dad. He split when I was nine. My mom is in California somewhere. Chasing after a man, I'm sure. She took off for good last year. Just picked up and left."

"I'm sorry."

"It's better, actually. Taking care of Mimi is much easier than dealing with her B.S."

He nodded and brushed a strand of hair away from her face, resting his hand on her neck. "What's your meeting about tomorrow?"

Tender. The man that had threatened to dismember Simmons on her behalf had such a soft side that made her fall even more.

The reality of their situation sucked.

"She has memory problems. I'm trying to get her into a special facility. But I've fought the insurance company every step of the way, and I can't afford to put her in one alone."

His hand lingered along her neck before it dropped to his side. No. It wasn't fair that Brogan sent those signals expecting her to do something about it. As much as she hated giving up control, he was in the driver's seat on this one. He held the rulebook in his back pocket.

"Let me know if I can help." He backed away, giving her air to breath. He began to button up his shirt. "The kitchen staff should be here soon. And my brothers."

"Early morning meeting?"

"Yes."

"I'll start on the advertising as soon as I can." She tapped the closed laptop sitting on his desk. "Do you mind if I take this home?"

"Not at all." He buttoned the cuffs of his shirt. "But don't concern yourself about it tomorrow."

"I should have time. The meeting is at ten thirty. I hope to take her for a tour after that, but it depends on what the insurance says. Can I swing by and pick the computer up after my shift today?"

"Sure. And let me know what they say about your granny's situation." He slipped his navy tie around his neck and began to tie it. She watched as she did every day. Couldn't help it. He glanced up once, his blue eyes snagging hers for a heartbeat before looking back down.

He reached out and took his suit coat from the back of his chair. And, as she'd done a few times, she stepped closer and straightened his already straight tie. Her hand smoothed the tie. She'd gotten bolder each time. She aimed dozens of signals Brogan's way. This time, she let her hands rest along his waist.

She tilted her head up. His chest rose and fell with a deep breath.

But he never made a move.

All they did was torture themselves.

"Well, this is interesting." Rian leaned against the door. Didn't knock. Didn't make a sound.

Brogan's work mask slipped over his face as he brushed past her and sat back down at his desk. "It's not interesting at all." He looked at his computer, flipping back to his email.

Selena stepped away, frustrated. "Don't worry. I'm about to leave so you can work, *Mr. O'Keeley.*"

Brogan's shoulders inched higher.

"Please, don't leave on my account," Rian said.

"I have work to do." She drummed her fingers on the closed laptop case. "I'll find you to get this when I'm leaving."

Brogan nodded without making eye contact. "Alright."

She sighed and passed by Rian. He shifted, blocking her way enough that she stopped. He winked. "Nice to see you, Selena." He held his arms out wide for a hug looking more mischievous than flirtatious. And she thought Cathal was the one up to no good most of the time. She gave him his hug. "Let me know the next time you plan on going out to the bar," he said.

"Rian—" Brogan grumbled.

He lowered his voice to barely a whisper. "Works every time." He released her, and she exited the room, feeling the eyes of both men on her back. What had Rian meant? What worked every time? Brogan made her mind a mess each morning when she left. She didn't need to add another Irishman to the confusion.

BROGAN STARED at Selena's text.

The insurance company fell through again. I have another meeting in 30 days. This sucks.

Figuring out what to do about her confused him more than he needed with the restaurant on the verge of closing.

"Are you with us, Brog?" Rian leaned over to look at his phone. "Ah. I see your mind is occupied."

Brogan tossed his phone to the low coffee table in front of them. "No. You don't see." Because they didn't see it his way. Didn't see the responsibility to ensure their future was secure. The fact they were grown men was beside the point. His Ma would expect him to do everything he could to keep the pub open. Keep them together.

Cathal reached forward, a glass of whiskey in his hand, and snagged the phone.

"You don't know the passcode," Brogan muttered. A second later, Cathal held up the phone, open to Selena's text. "Remind me to change it."

Cathal smiled as his finger swiped across the screen of Brogan's phone. "You need a lesson on how to text a woman."

"She's an employee."

"Who is upset, obviously. Go over there. Comfort her."

Rian sipped his Guinness. "You like her. Anyone that's

seen the two of you together lately knows that. You're trying to hide it, I know, but you're doing a pretty crappy job of it."

Brogan reached for his beer. Her earlier text had pushed him into having one for a change. "Fine. I'll admit it. I do like her."

"No shit," Cathal murmured.

"Spending each morning with her has solidified that I like her more than just the fact she's a pretty face. But it doesn't matter. I'm *not* crossing that line." His voice rose as if he needed his own conviction coming from his lips to actually control his body. Because it seemed like no matter what he told himself, it all disappeared the minute she came close to him. The way she straightened his tie. He had no idea if his tie was ever crooked and he didn't give a damn.

She wasn't trying to seduce him. He'd had that before with Crissy. Either Selena was a very talented actress, or she was just as nervous about crossing that line as he was. For his own sanity, he'd take that version for the time being.

"Alright. We get it. You're a saint."

"I'm not a saint." He hadn't had a saintly thought about Selena in several months.

"You have a lovely woman with golden eyes issue you a freaking invitation to make a move every single day, and you can walk away. She was two inches from being in your arms yesterday. Had her hands *on* you."

Cathal held up his drink. "That, dear brother, makes you a saint. We'll hold your canonization later. Back to the main business at hand. The loan. The bank agreed with certain stipulations. They want all three of our personal guarantees."

No doubt he'd give his guarantee. He'd do anything for the restaurant.

Rian wasn't as quick to answer. "I don't know. Can we find another bank and run it past them?"

Cathal tilted his head forward. "Damn it, man. Just put in or get out of the business."

Brogan laughed. "That's easy for you to say. Between the three of us, Rian's name is more important. No one cares about the man in the back that does the paperwork or you, whatever the hell it is you do most of the time, but they know Rian O'Keeley. If we don't make this work and him to be financially linked to a failing business—"

"He's right." Rian chuckled. "For once in that pretty head of his. I should go in without any reservations. I'll do it. Because I believe in us. In this restaurant."

Cathal nodded. "Hell, yeah."

"Then I'm in, too," Brogan said. "Not sure that any bank would want you once you give them your financial statement. You have more in student loan debt than assets."

Cathal shrugged. "Georgetown was expensive."

"Your lifestyle was expensive," Brogan shot back. "If we're all in, then there's only one more thing to do." He held out his bottle of beer, the other two men toasting with him. "Here's to O'Keeley's."

They all drank and set their empties on the coffee table. Rian leaned back, his long, lanky frame taking up a lot of space. "Glad that boring part is over. When are you going to make a move on Selena?"

"I'm not," Brogan snapped back. "Both of you, just drop it." The constant reminders didn't help the situation.

"No." Cathal leaned forward. "You've never found a woman like this. You look different when you're with her."

"Maybe it's just lust?"

Both his brothers looked at each other before Rian rubbed a hand over his mouth. "Lust, eh? No. You look far too unhappy for it to be just lust." He paused, always for effect. "You like her—really like the woman behind all that hair."

"And eyes. Those eyes get me," Cathal added.

Brogan growled. He felt it. Heard it. Didn't care that both his brothers smiled wider.

"There he is." Cathal rubbed his hands together. "You need this, Brogan. Keep it low key. There's no reason you can't move on Selena and not let it interfere with your work. She doesn't seem like the type to try and sleep her way to the top. She's not Crissy."

"No."

"To which part?"

Brogan took a deep breath. "She's not the type. I keep trying to put her in that light, and it's not fair to her. I know it." And, damn, he wanted to kiss her. Just once, give in to his urge to touch her without the fear that something bad would happen. He wanted to be selfish. Do something without thinking of the business first. Without thinking of what was best for his brothers.

And now, those same brothers, the ones who he'd walk away from Selena for, were pushing him straight into her arms. If anything bad happened now, it'd be on all of them.

Rian patted Brogan on the back. "Then go get her. It's a miracle the woman is still interested in you at this point; you are so hot and cold with her. I honestly thought the two of us were the last people on the earth that would put up with your moody ass, but for some reason, there she is. Fire her if you need to."

"That's been suggested before. I don't want to fire her. She's incredible at her job in the dining room. She's taking on helping with the advertising in the mornings. She's really good at that, too. I never thought I'd end up wanting someone to share the load with running this place, but she and I fit together."

"Fire her," Cathal said, a smile already brightening his face. "Then hire her back in the morning."

"I'm not sleeping with her. No matter what." He snapped out, more for himself than for Cathal.

"Your call." Cathal rose and pointed at Brogan's cell phone. "That fact remains that your woman needs someone tonight. If she's having to take care of her granny that way and was dealt a low blow, then she's sad." He looked at his watch. "It's eight thirty. Plenty of time for you to swing by the store, pick up some wine, and take it over to her."

"And you're the person that knows what I should do?"

Rian nodded. "Between the three of us, Cathal is definitely the best one for advice on women. He can lure them in and toss them back like he's fishing for sea bass."

"True." But getting past his own rules seemed impossible. He'd known Selena for almost seven months, closely for two weeks. She was beautiful and sweet. Funny. One night. One kiss. She wasn't Crissy. He'd prove that to himself.

8

I t'd been a while since he'd made a fool of himself. Brogan knocked lightly on Selena's apartment door and waited. He scanned the dark parking lot. He'd lived in Atlanta long enough to know there were worse places, shady areas of the town it wasn't safe to venture into after dark. The hair on the back of his arms stood up. Selena lived here. It was a step higher than a dump, really. Unsafe. He hated it.

He knocked again. Would she actually answer?

"Who is it? I'll call the cops."

"Please don't." He readjusted his grip on the wine as he heard several deadbolts and chains unlatching down the door. Her confused face appeared.

"Hi." Lame opening, but he already doubted his sensibility for showing up unannounced.

And to do what?

He held up the wine. "Your text sounded like you might need some cheering up."

She nodded, her eyes wide as she stepped back into her apartment.

"Is it alright I came over?" The insecurity rolling through his body didn't sit well. Only Selena made him feel that way. He couldn't separate it between the fear of rejection or the fear of making a big mistake when it came to trusting her—trusting his instinct. He would let down his guard, something he rarely did. He acknowledged that. But he had the wall built around him, keeping employees on one side, for a reason—a very sensible reason.

"Yes. Absolutely." She smiled, and his muscles relaxed. "Sorry. I would never have thought you'd come over." She looked at the clock on the wall. "And so late. You strike me as an early to bed, early to rise guy."

"I am." He scanned the small, cramped apartment. It wasn't dirty. Boxes of adult items, he guessed for her granny, were stacked in the corner. Selena's sneakers, the ones she wore when she worked, were underneath the coffee table.

Along with her flip flops. A few blankets and a pile of towels sat in one chair. And nothing matched. The furniture was old, maybe thirty or forty years.

"Did you bring that for me?" She tapped on the bottle.

"Yes. For us." He searched her face. No make-up. No pretense.

"The kitchen is over here." She turned and led the way. "I didn't think you drank. At least, I don't remember ever seeing you drink when your brothers do."

He set the wine on the counter. "I don't. Typically." He didn't like to lose control of himself. Enough embarrassing mornings after getting scuttered had developed the habit of only one or two drinks occasionally. But he needed one if he was going to keep pushing forward with Selena. He wanted to relax. Enjoy the moment.

She passed him a wine opener and pulled two glasses from the cabinets.

"Tell me about the insurance company," he said.

"Nothing to tell, really. They'll put her in a general care facility—a nursing home. But she needs more than that. I'm trying to get them to cover the cost of a different facility, but they keep saying she doesn't qualify, and they won't pay. So then I took her back to the doctor. He tried *another* medication." She made a circle in the air with her finger. "And the merry-go-round starts all over again. And I hate it when she changes meds. This one seemed to disorient her all over again, but it was just the first dose. That may change as her body adjusts."

"I'm sorry. I know that's frustrating." He poured them both a glass.

She stood there, waiting.

And he didn't know what to do. Should they stay in the kitchen and sit at the table? That's what a *friend* would do. Is that what she needed right then? A friend?

He ran a hand over his hair and looked around the kitchen. Worn furniture like the living room. He didn't expect a high class, chrome kitchen judging by the outside of the apartment complex, but he wished she had something a little better. He swallowed a sip of the wine as his next thought rammed into him. He wished he could give her better.

She smirked. "Would you like to go into the living room and sit down?"

"Sure." Good. He'd let her take the lead on this. He didn't want to have misread her signals. He took a sip of the wine as he sat down beside her, hating Crissy had screwed up his ability to sit next to a beautiful woman and not feel like he was still in grade school. Selena wasn't Crissy.

But if they did give in, and kissed, what happens tomorrow? They'd have to keep it a secret. He'd just fired those two employees for their supply room antics. He drank his wine, hardly tasting it, and thought about the moment with Selena in the same room. He might need to take that door off the hinges. Supply rooms were trouble for him, too.

Selena sipped her wine, watching him over the rim. He set his wine on the table and folded his hands in his lap. "I'm not sure this is a good idea." He could always leave. They hadn't crossed any line.

"Why did you come here?"

"I'm not sure."

She leaned forward and sat her wine glass beside his. "Can I be honest with you?"

He chuckled, releasing a little bit of his nervous energy. "Are you not usually?" No other employee talked to him the way she did.

"I hold quite a lot back, actually." She pursed her lips together. He'd give anything to know what thought ran through her mind. After a moment, she set her hand on his thigh.

His strong reaction to her confused the hell out of him. It wasn't something easy or simple between them. She was complicated in every way possible. With his job. With her granny. But right then, that disappeared.

"When we were in the supply room, and you held me if I'd kissed you, would you have kissed me back?"

He let go of his pride for a millisecond. "Yes." And then Katie would have discovered them. "But you work for me. I...this...." He couldn't even get it out.

She shifted closer. His saving grace was the hesitancy he saw in her eyes—the small amount of insecurity about pushing things forward so similar to his relieved him.

Could he really blame her? He found stupid reasons to

touch her when they were alone and then pushed her as far away as possible.

"So our job, that's the only thing that's bothering you?"

"What else would it be?"

She looked away for a moment, and he wished he knew what thoughts ran through her head.

"Brogan." She said his name and then sighed. Slowly, she reached up and skimmed her fingertips along the edge of his jaw. "I want to kiss you." Her eyes dropped to his lips. "And I'll make the first move, so you have no doubt that I want this as much as you do." Her bottom lip trembled slightly before she caught it with her teeth. "At least I hope that you do."

She leaned closer.

He did stop her, with a hand on her shoulder. "Selena." When he got his first taste of her, it wouldn't be with trepidation in her eyes. He'd bear the weight of it for both of them. He wanted this, and he'd make sure she knew it. "You're fired."

She blinked and started to pull away. "What?"

Then he kissed her, his lips taking away whatever question she started to ask. His hand slipped from her shoulder, along the slender curve of her neck and into her hair.

He tried to stay in control, but the heat kept slipping through with each little moan or movement she made to get closer.

Her hand gripped his wrist as if she had to hold on. The sweet wine on her tongue gave him a buzz, his head spinning with the effect.

Why had he even questioned this? The world clicked together. And that had never happened before. Not with any other woman. A first kiss shouldn't have this much power. Or significance.

"Mama?"

The word broke them apart. Selena closed her eyes a brief second before standing up from the sofa. There, her granny stood, in her faded nightgown looking disoriented. Her white hair stuck out at an odd angle, and she braced herself up on the wall.

"Give me a second, Brogan." Selena turned her granny around and helped her back to the room adjacent from them.

Selena's reality slammed into him. She didn't need this complication in her life. He wasn't a good bet, not being her boss. He could never give her anything more than this, secret meetings, only to treat her "normal" during the day. That would be torture. A distraction from his responsibilities to his brothers and their business. Unfair to her.

He rose and pulled his keys from his pocket. He'd wait until she came out, but then he'd leave before he messed their relationship up further.

It was hard as hell to walk away from that feeling of perfection.

"SELENA?" Mimi's eyes were unfocused, and she looked around the room wildly as she slipped back into reality. Selena would have to call the doctor in the morning and tell him.

"Yes. You're having a dream, Mimi. C'mon, I'll help you to the restroom and then back to bed." She walked Mimi back into the bedroom and to the bathroom. By the time she got her a drink of water, Mimi was fully coherent but tired. She climbed back into bed and rolled to face the wall.

Selena waited until she heard the light, steady breathing before leaving the room again. Only when she spotted Brogan, waiting by the front door, did she realize that she'd just up and left him.

"I'm sorry. You won't be the first guy to cut out when they see the reality of what I handle." She'd just hoped Brogan was different. Because, if he'd felt a quarter of the impact from their kiss, then he couldn't walk away.

His eyebrows shot down tight. "Cut out because of your granny? You think that's what I'm doing?"

"I don't know what you're doing." She didn't know what *she* was doing. She crossed her arms, feeling exposed. They'd shared an incredible kiss, one that'd been weeks in the making.

Sweet with a little edge underneath. As she'd expected, Brogan controlled it. For once, his need to be in charge had been precisely what she needed. She'd kissed men before, made the first move. Put herself out there. But not with someone like Brogan. God, she'd been nervous. Until their lips touched.

He sighed and ran a hand over his hair, disheveled. "I admire you for taking care of her this way."

"But? There's always a but."

"No buts. It's late. I was going to leave you to it, so you didn't feel the need to rush back out here to me."

"It's fine. I know having her here changes things." She hugged herself tighter, hating how petty she felt. Her voice sounded harsh in her ears. "We can just forget this happened if you want."

"Forget?" He blinked, his blue eyes cautious. "Is that what you want?"

She knew she didn't want a man that couldn't handle the fact this was her life at the moment. He took another step toward the door. Her heart fell to her stomach.

Better she found out now that he couldn't handle it than once her heart was really tangled up.

He paused and changed direction, taking three long steps to get to her.

Without warning, he tugged her head back by her hair as his lips met hers. His kiss struck through her body, straight to her toes.

Deep and sensual. Dominating.

She rose on her toes, wrapping her arms around his neck and craving as much as he'd give.

And he gave her plenty to remember him by.

She felt the frustration in his tense body. God, kissing this way, outside of marriage, was probably outlawed in at least twenty-seven countries.

His other hand, splayed across the small of her back, pressed their bodies tight, amping up the intensity of his control over the powerful kiss. Nothing resembled the controlled kiss on the sofa a few minutes earlier.

How was it the same man?

Brogan ended it with the same savagery that he'd started with. He released her hair and stepped away.

They were both out of breath, staring at one another, eyes wide. Part of her wished he'd toss her over his shoulder and cart her off to her bedroom, finish the caveman routine and end the misery.

Instead, he straightened his shoulders and took a solid, deep breath. "You're hired, again." He turned and walked out of the apartment, leaving her to put the pieces together that he'd shattered with that epic kiss. How had her life changed so dramatically in twenty minutes?

"The entire space is very nice," the loan officer at the bank said for the third time. The man looked younger than Cathal, near thirty, his suit too large on his skinny frame. His smooth skin probably didn't even see a razor every day.

"I'm glad you think so, Mr. Peters." Brogan subtly glanced at his watch. The unexpected visit occurred at eight thirty. Cathal sent a text early this morning informing Brogan he better cut his workout short and be dressed by the time the man showed up. They wanted to do an on-site interview before approving the loan.

"Good morning—" Selena pulled up short, the happy expression on her face shifting immediately to shock. "Jacob? What are you doing here?"

Jacob?

Mr. Peters' eyes brightened. "Selena. Goodness, it's been years."

And then they hugged.

Brogan crossed his arms as the hug lasting longer than necessary. "I see you know each other," he said, as a way of interruption. He'd hoped for his morning with Selena to consist of a talk about how they should handle the situation at work, seeing how he wanted only to lock the door and feast on her lips again. But *Jacob* had interrupted that.

And now he had his damn hands on her.

Jacob pulled away, his gaze never leaving Selena's face. "Yes. We dated while I was in college."

She looked just as pleased to see him. "What are you doing here?" She did glimpse, for a quick second, at Brogan before her attention went back to the man that held the fate of their loan in his hands. Hands that were still sitting possessively on Selena's waist from their hug.

Selena moved away, and Jacob followed her. "I'm a loan officer at the bank. Do you work here?"

She nodded. After another quick glimpse at Brogan, she beamed another smile at Jacob. "Mr. O'Keeley is my boss." Brogan hated the sharp way she said it. What did she want? For him to announce that she was his girlfriend or something? Girlfriend wasn't a title he'd use with Selena.

Just his.

It sounded possessive, even in his head, but that's how it'd felt last night. That last kiss he'd given her, lacking his usual restraint, had claimed her. He hadn't intended it to be that way.

Jacob looked at his watch. "It's a little early, isn't it?"

Smoothly she pulled out her laptop. "I help out in the office before my shift starts."

He smirked. "Doing what?"

Did she not catch the derisive way he asked that? Brogan's body tensed again when Jacob set a hand on her shoulder.

"She's the VP of Advertising." Brogan made up her job title on the spot. He'd wanted to say, "She's mine, back the hell off," but it might sabotage the bank loan to get in the young kid's face.

Selena watched Brogan for a full five seconds. He knew he should say something, but he couldn't. She had to know that.

Jacob sat on the edge of Brogan's desk, ignoring that he'd even spoken and leaning a little closer to Selena. "We need to get together and catch up."

Brogan's hands tightened into fists. He couldn't help it. He fought every primal instinct to stand there and not let him know that they were an item.

Because they weren't. He wasn't an idiot. One kiss didn't mean Selena had to drop any other man she saw for him.

"Ah, the gang's all here," Cathal said, strolling in with a large coffee in his hand. "Nice to see you again, Jacob."

"You, too. So, how about it, Selena? Go out with me tonight?"

Cathal's eyes shot to Brogan and back to Selena. "Well, what did I miss? I don't usually deal with loan officers who ask out our employees."

Selena stared at Cathal for a long, hard second. "Jacob and I used to date. I don't know, four years ago?"

Cathal shook his head and took a sip of his coffee, walking around the desk to stand beside Brogan. He didn't need his brother to tell him what he thought of the situation. He could see that eager puppy dog look on Jacob's face as easily as Brogan did.

Selena rose and pretended to fiddle with her laptop, putting Jacob to her side. She flicked her eyes up to Brogan. He wanted to drag her over the desk to him.

Cathal nudged Brogan before raising his voice. "Why don't we all go out tonight? Then we can meet about the loan, and you two can get reacquainted."

Jacob hesitated.

Until Cathal added, "how about Five-Seven-Nine? My treat."

His treat? That place was easily a $100 a plate before alcohol. Selena's mouth fell open for a quick second until Jacob leaned closer, his shoulder brushing hers. "Would you really be there?"

Brogan took a deep breath. He'd rather have Jacob there with Selena than to send them off on their own. "Yes. As our VP of Advertising, we'd want her there in case you had any questions on our future marketability."

Her eyes widened.

Jacob clapped his hands together. "Well, then that sounds like a date. Can I pick you up?"

Cathal stepped forward. "You know, she has to work an extra shift today, so we'll carpool from here. We can meet there at about six."

Looking to her for confirmation, or hope, Jacob waited for Selena to answer. She swallowed, pursed her lips together, and nodded. "Yes. That would be easier. We can catch up at dinner. Surely it won't all be about work."

"No," Brogan said, smiling even though it hurt his face to do it. "You can get reacquainted all you want."

"I'm looking forward to it. Thank you for the invitation, Cathal." He hugged Selena again without any invitation to do so. "I'm really happy we ran into each other."

"Me, too." She smiled as he left. They all stood in silence until they heard the front door to the restaurant close.

"What the hell?" She said, slamming the lid of her laptop closed.

At the same time, Brogan came around the desk. "You just let some guy put his hands on you like that?"

"We dated for three years. We talked about getting married at one point. He's not just *some guy*."

"But you aren't together now."

She crossed her arms, eyes flashing with heat. "No. Now, I'm just the VP of Advertising. What kind of bullshit is that, Brogan?" she shouted.

"It's the kind that will hopefully make sure we even still have a restaurant next year."

"Oh!" She took a step closer, her finger pointing at him. "So now you're using me to soften up the loan guy?"

He ran a hand through his hair and paced away and then back to her. "How in the hell was I supposed to know that you two knew each other?" He fired back. "It's not like any of this was planned."

"Then why did you invite me to dinner if it wasn't to help you out?" Her voice raised to match his.

He stalked toward her until they were an inch apart. "Because I'd sure as hell rather watch you and he become reacquainted than to imagine what happens when you go on a date with another man."

"You know being exclusive with someone, Brogan, means you call them something other than your damn VP of Advertising."

The argument put a flush in her cheeks he'd not seen before. Her lips parted as she took a deep breath.

He didn't want to yell. So, he kissed her, hard, expecting her to push him away.

And she did. But only for a brief second. The anger in her eyes had faded. She fisted her hands into his dress shirt and tugged him close, kissing him the rough way he needed at that moment.

She was his. Every inch of his body recognized her as his

mate. A counterpart that kept him balanced. And she shouldn't even be in his arms.

"Thank the Lord," Cathal muttered from the sofa. "You guys are too loud this early in the morning with all your shouting."

Brogan looked over Selena's head as she turned to look, too. His brother had one arm thrown over his eyes, sprawled out across the sofa. At least he'd faked not being hungover for Jacob.

Selena moved away. "I guess I need to call the nurse to see if she can stay or call Katie's sister."

"I'm sorry to involve you in this." He wanted to drag her back, kiss her again, and prove that she was his.

The feeling of insecurity creeping in around a woman put an uncomfortable feeling in his chest. He put himself back into control. Distant and safe.

"Let me know about those advertising sites when you get around to checking on them. And there's a delivery today that is supposed to arrive before the kitchen staff. Keep an ear out for that."

Her open expression closed off again. "Got it." And she left, taking everything she'd brought into his office with her.

"You suck at dating," Cathal mumbled from the sofa. "I'm surprised you've ever had a ride the way you blunder things up."

"I didn't ask for your opinion." He sat down at the desk, pulling up his to-do list for the day. Reminders about payments and payroll information, boring, ordinary things that he could focus on instead of Selena.

Cathal sat up, squinting, reaching for his coffee cup. "No. You'll shoot yourself in the foot and lose Selena before you ask for help."

"I don't need help. And you can go back to your bed anytime you want to."

Cathal shook his head. "Oh, no. I plan on staying. The entire day. I need to make sure you don't royally screw everything up with that sweet girl out there."

"Why is my relationship with her any of your business?"

"Because, dear older brother, if you act like a jerk much longer, Rian and I are going to kick you out of the family and adopt her." Cathal left, slamming the door behind him.

Great. Everyone was against him. Why? All he'd done is treat Selena like an employee. He may have deeper feelings for her, but it didn't mean they didn't have a business to run. Kissing her senseless before ordering her about might have been a little extreme. He hadn't lied to her, though. He couldn't stand the thought of Jacob taking her out on a date.

SELENA HEARD the door slam shut. Seriously? How did Brogan have any reason to be angry in this situation? She turned, saw Cathal, wide awake, striding across the restaurant. She'd set up her laptop at a table near the front, as far away from Brogan as possible.

The temptation to go back in there, soothe it over, was too great. She didn't have anything to apologize for.

VP of Advertising her ass.

"Darling," Cathal began, pulling out a chair. "I came to apologize on behalf of my family."

She rolled her eyes. "Brogan can dig himself out of this one, but thanks."

"Not for Brogan." He sat down. "For me. Rian. And my Ma and Da. We've let him fester into this controlling arse that can't see beyond his own nose." He patted her hand. "I told him that we were going to kick him out of the family and adopt you."

She laughed. "I bet he didn't like that. Is that why he slammed the door?"

"I slammed the door. Which didn't help the headache." He took a sip of his coffee. "He's not the only one with a temper. I've just learned to control mine." He winked. "Most of the time."

Her laptop played the welcome music. She typed the login information and sat back while it finished booting up.

Cathal stared out the front window. "Tell me. How close were you and Jacob?"

It seemed so long ago. Four years. She was twenty-four and thought life would be wonderful. On her own. No responsibility. But the way Jacob had treated her still hung around. Still made her question her worth.

"Close. Three years. But, he wanted someone with a little more class than I had. Or have." She picked at her nails, hating to relive the emotions. He'd hidden her away, gave her the insecurity she fought long and hard to overcome. Like she wasn't worthy of his friends or society.

He chuckled. "You were the one that got away."

"Not sure I'd rate myself that high."

"Don't sell yourself short. After all, you are the VP of Advertising."

She snorted. "Yeah. Because that's a better title than girlfriend."

"Brogan is stupid." Cathal winked. "You could always demand the money that comes with a title like that."

"No." She shook her head, at least sure of that. "I'm not going to leverage any part of this relationship."

The buzzer near the front door rang. "That would be the

delivery." Cathal stood up, finished his coffee, and tossed the cup into the small trash can behind the hostesses' desk.

Selena rose to handle the delivery, but he held up his hand. "Sit. Do the advertising thing. I've devoted myself to staying here for the day and going to dinner. Might as well do something useful."

"Thanks." She watched him disappear down the long hallway to the kitchen. His brothers didn't give him enough credit. Cathal was smart. He just didn't have any focus because they treated him like a kid. He played the part.

Rian opened the front door, a sour look in place.

She hitched her thumb over her shoulder. "Your bossy brother is in his office. Cathal's on the loading dock."

He blinked, giving her a small smile. "Good morning to you, too, Selena. And here I thought my morning was rotten, but something obviously irked you more. Or someone."

"The latter, but I won't waste your time with it." She relaxed her shoulders. "Do you want to talk about your morning?"

"Not really. But I received an interesting text message from Brogan telling me we're to go to dinner at Five-Seven-Nine tonight with the banker." He crossed his arms. "And that you'll be joining us."

"I would ask if you disapprove, but it was Brogan's idea. You know, to have his VP of Advertising there."

Rian smirked and looked exactly like Cathal for a moment. "A promotion?"

"No. A way to make sure Jacob didn't have a clue that Brogan and I have a relationship if you'd call it that." Because as far as she was concerned, what they had was a big mess.

"Jacob?"

Selena set her hands in her lap. She hated the testiness

in her voice. "My ex-boyfriend and your banker. He asked me out to get reacquainted."

"In front of Brogan?"

"Yes. It was Brogan's idea for the group date tonight. That was after he introduced me as his VP of Advertising." Dumb title.

Rian ran a hand over his mouth.

"I'm glad it makes you laugh."

"No." He shook his head. "It makes me incredibly angry at my brother on your behalf that he wouldn't acknowledge what you have together."

"Cathal already threatened to kick him out of the family and officially adopt me."

Rian stepped over and kissed her on the forehead. It was completely platonic, but it eased a lot of her frustration at the situation. People supported her. That was a new position to find herself in. Newer than even VP of Advertising. She was usually supporting the people around her, helping her mom through a constant string of disastrous relationships, and now taking care of Mimi.

"Absolutely." He stalked away, taking long strides to the office door, opening it without knocking.

Selena chewed on her bottom lip. If she ever got back to the point where she *wanted* to kiss Brogan again, she'd have to remember to lock it.

Shaking her head, she pulled up the list of websites and publications that Brogan mentioned wanting the advertising to run. The title might have been a lame way to cover up their relationship, but she'd be the best damn VP of Advertising possible. Seeing Jacob brought back the shame and frustration she'd felt when he'd broken it off the first time. The distance made their break-up an easy excuse.

But when she looked at the future with Jacob, she could only see the power difference between them.

He had a college education. A good-paying job. Back then, he had aspirations to run a bank someday. And she had nothing. No degree. No prospects. And he let her know it.

Is that why Brogan's flip-flop treatment bothered her so much? A headache started along the base of her skull, radiating upward as reality slammed into her. She'd ended it once because she felt as though she wasn't someone's equal. She and Brogan were headed in the exact same direction.

10

Brogan refused to pace. Waiting on Selena to arrive at the swanky restaurant killed him. Jacob sat at the bar, sharing a drink with Cathal and Rian. He'd expected them to all come together, based on the carpool idea from that morning, but Selena wanted to go home and shower and change.

He'd ridden with Cathal, hoping to have a chance to soothe over their fight, but he'd not engaged in any conversation. Rian, on the other hand, had talked non-stop to him all day. About nothing important. Just there. Talking. Bothering him. And the more irritated Brogan had become, the more Rian talked.

Their treatment was intentional. His brothers knew precisely how to annoy him and make a situation worse. He wanted to brood in silence. Or grab the first opportunity he could find to be alone with Selena. But they'd prevented that as well.

Selena's car pulled up to the curb. The valet jogged around, opening her door, a broad smile on the man's face as he helped her out of the vehicle.

Brogan's stomach tightened, and his hands flexed.

She walked around the car, those sexy high heels she'd worn at the bar the other night, giving her a few extra inches. A black dress stopped short in the front fell to the bottom of her thighs in the back. She'd mentioned she never exercised, but her long, legs were toned from spending hours waiting tables.

She'd left her hair down, pulled over one shoulder, exposing her neck and collarbone on one side of the off the shoulder dress.

She stopped three feet away instead of walking straight into his arms where he wanted her.

"Close your mouth, Brogan," she said, a cute smile on her lips. "But I appreciate the unspoken compliment."

"You look amazing." And Jacob would have the opportunity to drool over her as well.

"Thank you." She tilted her head to the side. "Too bad about being the VP of Advertising right now."

He cleared his throat. "Yes, it is." His voice deepened, and he didn't care about his accent sounding thick. "But later, Selena. If you can forgive me for acting like a complete jerk this morning. Watching another man touch you drove me insane."

"Selena!" Jacob held the door open to the restaurant. The pup's eyes raked over her body.

Brogan fisted his hands in his pockets.

She didn't glance back his direction, her eyes locked on Jacob as she walked to him.

Brogan turned to follow, careful to keep his eyes averted from her body.

With her arrival, the host picked up menus and led the way through the restaurant to a seat in the back.

Cathal spoke, his voice low and oddly serious. "Not sure

this was the best idea. It's hard to swallow watching another man touch her that way, and she's not my woman. Are you going to be alright?"

Brogan would rather witness it than to live in his imagination for them to go out alone.

"I'll sit beside him," Cathal whispered. "You sit beside her." He nudged him. "But keep your hands to yourself."

Impossible.

"Maybe I should sit across the table—"

Rian appeared on Brogan's other side. "And scare off our loan officer with that murderous look? I'll sit across from him." Before Brogan answered, the host began to pull out the seat for Selena, but Jacob took over.

Rian grunted. "I suddenly agree with Cathal. You might not make it through the night."

The three of them paused, waiting to see where Jacob sat.

Selena watched the three of them, her eyes narrowing until Jacob sat down beside her. As planned, they each took their seat.

She busied herself with her napkin, cutting her eyes in Brogan's direction. Had she forgiven him? He'd hold off giving her another apology at the moment. He still had to make it through dinner without making her mad, which wasn't likely with his current track record. Then he could apologize for everything at once.

But he did have one change to make. He leaned close, barely whispering his request. "Can you switch your hair to the other shoulder?" Because she might not be his date, but she sure as hell wasn't Jacob's date, and between the two of them, he wanted the best view possible.

Her lips twisted to the side, her small dimple appearing. As if on cue, she leaned her head back and pulled the length to the other side. With her cheek, neck, and shoulder exposed, Brogan picked up the menu. Great. He was a glutton for punishment. But at least he had the best view in the restaurant.

Rian shook his head, sending Brogan a sympathetic look. Someday, a woman would drive him to do stupid things as well.

"Welcome to the Five-Seven-Nine. I'm Luke and will be your waiter. Can I start you with something to drink?"

Jacob sat straight and began to talk as though he were in charge. "Do you have a wine list?" He looked at Selena. "Do you still enjoy white wine? I'll order for you like before."

"I do, yes. But," she said, pausing and looking at Cathal. "I think I'll let Cathal order my drink. My tastes have changed slightly."

His younger brother grinned with pride. "She'll have a Salt and Honey, with the Eighteen Reserve Jameson's."

"You drink whiskey now?" Jacob's use of the word like it was dirty pulled a quick smile from Rian's lips. "Here?" Jacob shook his head like he didn't agree. "Maybe a glass of wine with dinner?"

"Definitely. But, if you don't mind, I'd like Rian to pick the wine." She took a sip of her water.

The waiter stood by, observing the passive-aggressive power play she'd set up.

Brogan's shoulders relaxed. Maybe he could make it through dinner after all.

Jacob sat back in his chair and nodded his head toward Rian. "You're the cook, right?"

The amused smile dropped from Rian's face.

Hell.

Rian pushed back from the table and stood, buttoning his suit jacket. They always teased Brogan that he was the control freak. Couldn't sit back and relax. Both his brothers had specific triggers, per se, that lit the same intensity Brogan felt about the restaurant.

For Rian, it was anyone doubting his resume or ability. He'd fought for years to be recognized internationally. He regularly traveled, and nothing or nobody would ever come between him and his goals.

For Cathal, it was the way men treated women. They gave Cathal a hard time, but it kept them all from remembering the hell he'd been through. One of the main reasons they'd moved away from Ireland. Beating a man to death changed someone inside.

"Luke," Rian said. "If you wouldn't mind leading me toward the kitchen."

"What?" Jacob asked over Luke's confusion.

"Lead the way." Rian motioned Luke along.

Luke looked at Jacob. "Sir, did you want something to drink to start?"

"A glass of pinot grigio. Whatever brand is fine."

Brogan leaned his elbows on the table, aware his arm sat close to Selena's. "I'll have a glass of the Eighteen Year Reserved Jameson's as well. No salt or honey."

Rian left with Luke.

Jacob shifted, facing Selena. "Why would he go to the kitchen?"

She shrugged, her delicate shoulder lifting. Brogan had an overwhelming urge to kiss the smooth, exposed skin.

"Do you know any history about Rian O'Keeley?" she asked.

"He puts the menu together at your pub."

Brogan and Cathal shared a glance. They had to cater to this man to secure a loan, and he had no clue about their restaurant or the prestige that Rian carried.

Selena apparently took offense for the entire family. "Jacob, Rian is a really famous chef. You just called him an everyday cook. That's why I thought he'd be better suited to pair wine with my meal."

"But I know what you like," Jacob cooed, setting his hand on top of hers.

Cathal rolled his eyes.

Brogan swallowed down the shout, building in his chest.

Selena smiled sweetly. "I know, and I do like white wine, but my tastes have changed in four years. I'm sure yours have as well."

"That's why we need to go out, just the two of us, and get to know each other." Jacob knocked on the table. "It's settled. Next weekend."

Despite his brother's warning, Brogan set a hand on Selena's thigh underneath the tablecloth. Her dress had ridden up, though, and he unexpectedly touched her bare skin.

She sat up a little straighter and cleared her throat. "We can talk about it later. I have to check my schedule."

"Surely, Mr. O'Keeley could lose you for one night."

"I just don't know right now, Jacob. I have a lot going on in my life."

Brogan brushed his thumb along the side of her thigh before releasing it. Their drinks arrived. The whiskey didn't cool his throat, but the warmth of the alcohol eased the tightness in his muscles.

Jacob changed tactics, bringing up the fun they'd had when they dated the first time. His stories went on and on, downright boring Cathal judging by his brother's blank stare.

But they amused Selena. Her laugh didn't sound fake.

Brogan wanted to make her laugh that way. He'd never held that goal with a woman before.

Rian reappeared as Luke did.

"If you're interested, Jacob, Pierre will fix a special dinner for the four of us." Rian sat and glanced at Luke. "He'll inform you of the drink pairing as the courses arrive."

Luke recovered well and looked to Jacob. "Are you ready to order, or would you like me to inform the head chef that you'll accept the same menu?"

"I'm up for a surprise." Jacob nudged Selena. "If you are?"

"I trust Rian," she said with complete pride.

What Cathal had said was true. If Brogan didn't figure out this situation, they might very well kick him out of the family and keep Selena.

Brogan's cell phone buzzed in his pocket. He pulled it out.

We need to get him to talk about the loan. Not his pathetic dates from the last decade.

Cathal's hands rested in his lap, concealing his phone.

Brogan texted back.

I'll try to get Selena away. Then you engage.

Cathal nodded his head once.

If you can't beat out Jacob and win her, then I'm not sure I can call you my brother.

Brogan narrowed his eyes. But he had to agree. He had no plans to lose Selena to Jacob. He leaned closer to her as he began to stand and whispered, "Follow me." He left, walking to the hallway that held the restrooms. A quick look into another room revealed the restaurant's supply room.

Fitting.

"What?" Selena asked as she approached thirty seconds later.

Brogan opened the supply room door and motioned her in. She passed him, her eyes laced with curiosity. He closed the door behind them.

She crossed her arms. "Cute. The supply room? I'm not going to kiss you right now. My lips will be all swollen, and he'll know."

For the moment, he didn't care, but she was right. "Cathal wanted to approach the topic of the loan with the bank, try to get him to commit verbally."

"Yeah. I think he's more interested in trying to ask me out again."

"I hope you'll decline his offer." He slowly pushed her up against the back of the supply room door and locked the doorknob as he pressed his lips softly to the column of her neck.

The view he'd tortured himself with all night was his to savor.

"This is so not fair." Her hands slipped underneath his jacket, gripping the back of his shirt. "I can't even kiss you because I'd probably get lipstick all over your shirt."

"Then," he murmured, moving across her bare shoulder, "just stand there."

"That's no fun." Her head fell back. "How long are we supposed to stay gone?"

"Shh, I need another second." He worked his way back across her collarbone, breathing in that wildflower scent. With a mind of their own, his fingers skimmed along the edge of her skirt and the exposed skin of her thighs. Wanting a little more, he slipped his hands just underneath the hem.

"Brogan?"

He tightened his hands with the whisper of his name.

This was why he didn't drink whiskey. He stopped, his lips hovering over hers. Her hands tightened on his shirt.

As light as he could make it, he pressed his lips to hers. "Alright. I think I'll survive now."

"Yeah, but I don't know how I'm going to walk in these heels with my legs feeling like jelly."

Brogan patted her hip and then released her from the door. "Take a second in the powder room if necessary. I'll head back to the table."

He opened the door and checked the hallway. He took a step only to have Selena tug him back. Her deep kiss tasted sweet from her drink and ended as soon as it'd began.

"Now, I'll survive." She brushed past him and disappeared into the ladies' room.

He adjusted his tie and wiped any lipstick from his mouth as he proceeded back to the table. He sat down, Jacob's eyes on him immediately.

"Sorry about that," Brogan said, holding up his cell phone. "The shift manager had a question. Where's Selena?"

Jacob relaxed back in his chair. "Restroom. We were discussing financing options."

Cathal grinned and lifted his glass in Brogan's direction. "Yes. It seems Mr. Peters thinks the restaurant is worth the loan."

11

Selena didn't make it to work by nine, so her late greeting with Brogan was polite and informal and pissed her off again. She'd helped make sure Jacob had a lovely time. She engaged in conversation and lived up to be a *great* VP of Advertising. He should have greeted her with something more than a head nod. Despite the fact, other employees had arrived.

Katie jutted a hip out and rolled her eyes. "Why won't you go back out with me? I promise I'll be sober this time." Her eyes widened. "Unless you're seeing someone."

Selena whipped her head up. "What makes say that?"

Katie pointed at a spot on her neck. "Because that looks like a hickey."

"A hickey?" Crap. That would have been part of the supply room seduction.

"Who is it?" Katie leaned on the table. "Is it that Jacob guy you mentioned stopped by yesterday? You know, your old boyfriend?"

"No. I'm not interested in going out with Jacob again.

Last night proved that I've changed since we dated." For the better. She used to love his attention back then. Let him order things at restaurants for her because she was scared she'd mess it up. Now, she knew what she wanted. She also knew that giving the other men at the table decision making power would put them in a different light in Jacob's mind. He was always impressed with superiors. And it'd worked. Jacob sent over the loan papers to be signed that morning.

Brogan stood at the bar with Cathal. Both were in suits. Both attracting every female's attention in the place, including hers.

"It's the boss man, isn't it?"

"What?" Selena glanced around. "Be quiet. I don't want to get fired for your jokes."

"I wasn't joking." She shrugged. "Just the way you watch him. If he doesn't know you have the hots for him, the rest of us do."

Had she really been doing that? She turned her back to where Brogan stood. "Well, I'm not, and I don't. Granted, he is handsome. You've said that yourself."

"Yes. I have. So," Katie said, clasping her hands together, "if you're not seeing him, and that's *not* a hickey, then you have no reason not to come out with me."

Selena's jaw hurt from clenching. Brogan would *kill* her if he thought anyone was suspicious, and their jacked-up relationship would end before she had a chance to figure out where it could lead. At the moment, it wasn't likely to lead anywhere. She didn't want to be the secret girlfriend. She'd done that with Jacob, and it'd sucked.

"I'll go. But, I'm not wearing those shoes again. My feet hurt for a week afterward." Just like they did from wearing them the night before. But it'd been worth it to see the look on Brogan's face when she stepped out of her car.

"Deal. And I promise this time I'll stay sober."

"I might have to have a ride on speed dial."

She nudged her and winked. "Uh, huh. Like your dream boyfriend, *Brogan?*"

"This is interesting."

Selena froze with Brogan's voice from behind her.

Katie's eyes grew large. "I...I...I'm sorry, Mr. O'Keeley. I didn't see you. I was joking—"

"Stop. I think you're both talking instead of serving your customers." Brogan's thick Irish made Selena grimace. He was angry, and it showed.

She slowly turned around. His blue eyes narrowed to slits. But she wouldn't let him think Katie knew anything.

"Katie asked me to go back out to the bar with her." Selena continued even though Brogan crossed his arms and started to speak. "And she was *joking* about you showing up and driving me home last time. Because Cathal drove her home."

The muscle in his jaw jumped, but his shoulders relaxed by a fraction. Good.

"I would caution you against relying on others for a ride home." He held her gaze a beat longer than was probably normal. She looked away. If he didn't want to let everyone know, then he needed to get his emotions under control.

"Get back to work." He left, without a second look back, stalking to his office.

The door shut harder than necessary.

"Damn," Katie started, "you are so going out with me Saturday night and finding a guy. Screw him for making us feel like crap." She stuck her tongue out at Brogan's closed door.

"That's mature," Cathal said. He pulled out a chair and sat down with his cup of coffee. "And probably deserved."

Katie smirked. "I am going to get back to work."

Cathal didn't move. "What did I miss?"

"A misunderstanding that can't be discussed."

Brogan acting like a jerk again.

Every inch of Selena wanted to reassure Brogan that Katie was joking.

The restaurant door opened. Rian stalked through the dining room, moving quicker than usual. He scanned the room, his eyes landing on her and Cathal.

Cathal sipped his coffee. "Well, he looks a little upset."

"That's an understatement."

Rian dipped his chin in acknowledgment and then walked to Brogan's door and walked right in, shutting it behind him.

Strange.

"Let me go fix whatever is the problem now." Cathal left, following Rian's lead and walking into the office.

Katie bumped her. "All three bosses have now witnessed you standing around. Go do something, Selena."

She moved then, bussing tables and asking various customers if they needed anything for the next hour without any O'Keeley emerging from the office.

Cathal's voice behind her made her jump. "I need to put in a lunch order." He didn't flirt or wink. "And you need to bring it in when it's ready. I don't want to deal with anyone else at the moment." He shook his head. "Whatever happened earlier put Brogan in a massively shitty mood."

She pursed her lips for a moment before pulling a pad of paper from her back pocket to take his order. "He's my boss. I get that. But he's going to have to trust that I'm not going to run my mouth."

"You should tell him that. But not right now. We have

some planning to do and need nourishment. Three fish and chips. Three Guinness."

"Three?"

"Believe me. Between you and the bank shit, Brogan needs one or else we really will kick him out of the O'Keeley's this time."

She smiled.

"Ah. I can see that it makes you happy."

"No." Not happy. A little pleased that he had reacted to her. He flipped so quickly between being the boss in the Armani suit without a heart, to the man that brought wine to her to cheer her up and seduced her in supply closets. "I'm not happy he's upset."

Cathal set his hand on her shoulder. "Despite him being an arse most of the time, he is a good man."

"I know that, too." She looked up and met Cathal's gaze. "We're just trying to figure it all out, I suppose. He thinks this is one-sided. I'm flat out lying to one of my best friends. It sucks all around."

Cathal nodded. "Right. I get it." He tapped her pad with their orders. "One thing at a time, *mavourneen*." He walked back to the office, leaving her wondering what he'd just called her.

She scooted around behind the bar to put in the orders and pour the drinks. If Cathal thought it was one-sided, Brogan probably did, too.

She hated to do this, but if he wanted it to remain a secret, then she had no choice but to go out with Katie. She'd go to a bar. Have fun. Not flirt and not go home with anyone. Easy.

But he couldn't get mad. Like he'd done with Jacob. She wouldn't expect him to just stay locked inside if the situation was reversed and he had to appear as though he was still single. Besides, as she told him before, a title like VP of Advertising didn't earn him exclusivity rights over her.

Jacob had hidden her away before. And she'd let him. Brogan would never have that power over her.

She took the tray of food and drinks to the door of the office. She knocked twice and waited.

Brogan opened the door. His serious face faltered a moment when his eyes locked with hers. Yes. She threw a massive wrench into his perfect life.

"Come in," he said, stepping back. After a half-second hesitation, if that, maybe only a breath of a moment, he took the heavy tray.

She stood there, empty arms, as he carried it across the room and sat it on the coffee table.

As soon as Brogan's back was turned, Cathal grinned and gave her two thumbs up. Rian shook his head and snagged a fry off of a plate.

"I need to talk to you," he said and motioned toward the bathroom in the back she'd never been in before—the one he used to clean up after his workout each morning.

She turned on her heel and walked into the room, hearing the door shut behind them. It wasn't large. About the size of her bathroom in her small apartment. Clean. Nothing on the counter. One drawer on the side. Absolutely the opposite of the current state of her own bathroom with her blow dryer sitting in the sink and makeup everywhere.

The air smelled fresh with the hint of the aftershave she'd learned he used.

"Selena—"

"No." She held up her hand. She didn't want to fight. Not with him. Not over this. "I told you the truth. Katie has always teased me about you." Facing him, she was a little shocked to see the aggravated look on his face. "You're hot. I didn't just form that opinion about you in the last forty-eight hours since we kissed. You see the way she acts about Cathal. She always jokes about it."

He slipped his hands in his pockets.

"And it's put me in a crappy situation. I'm lying to her, swearing we aren't whatever the hell we are or aren't, and then hoping you believe me."

"I believe you."

"Great. Then?" she asked, pausing a moment and holding her hands out. Why had he wanted her in here?

He stalked toward her. She held her ground until he pushed the back of her thighs against the edge of the counter next to the sink. "I thought, when I first walked up, that you'd told her."

"I know." And it pissed her off, but she kept her silence. He had to work through something in his mind. His eyes scanned over her face, searching for an answer.

He stepped closer, his hips pressing hers until he picked her up by her thighs and set her on the counter. This Brogan she could handle.

He gripped the back of her knees, pulling her as tightly against him as possible. He tilted her face up but didn't kiss her. He looked at her like he tried to see inside. She didn't hide anything from him. Never had. Never would.

She cupped his face, skimming her fingers along his temple. "What is it, Brogan? Just tell me." She kissed him lightly, trying to ease his frustration. Maybe to ease her own.

"I don't want you to go out to the bar."

She wanted to smile, really, at the small amount of insecurity he'd shown. Brogan, literally, the hottest guy she'd ever seen, had her legs wrapped around his waist, holding her. He was scared of her going to a bar with Katie.

"I don't know how to get out of it, now. I told her I would

just to cover for her thinking we were together." Selena straightened his already straight tie. "I didn't know what else to do. I think it would look worse if I didn't go at this point."

"I don't want another man touching you." His hands squeezed her thighs, tugging her closer. "I don't think I could stand it again."

His breathless intensity almost made her come unhinged. She kissed him hard and deep. This was what she wanted from him. Commitment even if he couldn't say the words.

She broke it off just as quick. "Is that a request for your VP of Advertising to work exclusively for you?"

"Absolutely." His lips twisted to the side. "So what are you going to do about Katie."

"I'm going to go to the bar with her."

"But...."

"Going out with a friend doesn't mean I'm going to go home with another man. We might need to keep this under wraps for a little bit, I'll try to understand that, but I'm not going to hide-out at home, waiting for you to decide when we can see each other. I did that once before."

"With Jacob?"

"Yes. I'm not doing it again."

"What will you do if you're not there to pick up guys?"

She smiled and slipped her hands into his perfect hair. "Watch Katie hit on guys—or girls. I'm not sure what bar we're going to yet. And think of you." She nipped at his bottom lip. "And wish you could be there, in public, with me."

"I don't know if that will ever happen."

Ever? Would she forever remain his secret girlfriend? She ignored the deep ache growing in her stomach from the thought. He couldn't have meant it like that. She'd just told him about Jacob hiding her. Why would he think she'd ever go back to playing the role of a secret girlfriend?

"We need to get back to your brothers."

"I'm pretty sure they know about us."

"Well, I know I'm wasting your time." She needed some air. Space. He'd easily announced that he'd keep her hidden in the closet, away from the world, forever. She deserved more than that. She'd watched her mom be used, tossed around by men growing up. And, after Jacob practically did the same thing, she'd sworn she wouldn't ever chase after a man that way again.

But she wanted Brogan. She'd try to understand for a little bit longer.

"No. Never a waste of time."

"Well, you at least have more important things to do than wrap me around your waist." She held up her hand. "Okay, bad example for both of us." She pushed him back with a little nudge and hopped down. "Go figure out how to save your restaurant. They're here to meet with you. You can wrap me around you anytime."

"Is that a promise?"

She draped her arms around his neck, putting on a happy face even though her heart hurt. "Absolutely."

12

H ell.
　　Brogan read the purchase agreement from the owner of his property. A full five hundred thousand higher than the original offer.

"And he increased the price, because?"

Brogan passed the contract back to Cathal, his jovial brother quiet for a moment.

"Simmons came in with a higher offer. He said it was hard not to accept the offer right then, but he wanted to give us a chance."

"But another five hundred?" Brogan ran a hand over his hair, not caring how it looked. He stood in his condo, staring out over the Atlanta skyline. For fifteen years he'd lived in Atlanta. For the past ten operated the bar. Everything he had was wrapped up on the bar.

"I know. It was that shit Simmons pulled with Selena and our reaction. It's a power play."

He glanced over his shoulder, Cathal slowly shaking his head. They didn't have to say it out loud. Neither one of them would have done a thing different. They'd both want to beat the bastard to a bloody pulp. They'd both resisted.

Their Ma would be proud of that.

As it was, both he and Rian were very proud of Cathal for only snatching him away from Selena and not going further. Cathal's aggression, when it came to men like Simmons, wasn't controlled.

"We ask the bank for more." Brogan knew that was an impossible request.

Cathal tossed the paper onto the kitchen table and leaned back in the old, wooden chair. The sky rise condo building was modern, but not the furnishings inside Brogan's home. He'd brought over the table and chairs from his parents' house back in Ireland. Several pieces of furniture, in fact. Warm. That was how he wanted to live.

Rian lived with hardly any furniture. Everything chrome, black or white, and sparse.

Cathal was lucky his cleaning lady didn't quit.

"I already called Jacob Peters. He didn't say 'no' but he wasn't optimistic. I had half a thought to see if Selena could ask him for it." He held up his hands at Brogan's sharp look. "Hey, she's not my girl, and I hated seeing him make a fool of himself over her that way. He tried to cut up her steak."

"I think Rian was more appalled that he asked for ketchup to dip his in."

Cathal grinned. "By the end of the night, Rian hated his face more than you, if that was possible. Did you notice Rian left, without even saying goodbye?"

"No. Where is he now?" Brogan couldn't keep up with the restaurant and his brother's travel schedule.

"Not with a woman." Cathal shook his head. "He could wine and dine any woman on this planet, and instead, he lives like a monk."

Brogan chuckled at his brother's analogy. "You know he's not a monk. He doesn't feel the need to share the women he's interested in because then we'll want to meet them."

"Great." Cathal threw his arms up. "Our own brother is embarrassed by us."

"Probably." He motioned to the paper sitting on the table. "What are we going to do about that?"

"I've given it a little bit of thought. What about raising it through the restaurant? We have five more weeks before the owner needs a decision. Let's do something unique that draws in a crowd."

Brogan partway smiled. "We'd have to pay for someone to come in and plan the event. None of us know how to do that."

"What about Selena? You did give her that fancy title."

Brogan turned back to face Cathal. "What about her?" He checked his watch. "She's probably getting ready to go out to a bar with Katie."

"You have to trust her, Brog."

"I know." It didn't mean he had to like it.

"Do you want me to head out later and check-in with her?"

Brogan hesitated. "Does it make me an odd person if I said, 'yes,' and had you do it?" Because he did want to make sure she was safe. He trusted her not to be with another man. He didn't trust the other men out there. Selena was beautiful. Simmons and Jacob confirmed that she was attractive to everyone else as well.

"Yes. It makes you very sad."

"I'll take sad. Text me that she's alright."

Cathal nodded once. "I will. Do you think she could plan an event like that? You said yourself she's smart."

He took a breath and pulled out the chair opposite his

brother and sat. "She is smart. I don't know if she'd do it, though. I could ask her. But what kind of event?"

"I'd say stick to our strongest qualities."

"Fighting?"

Cathal's quick smile eased some of the tension between them. "Better. I don't know why we don't make Rian do something. He just had an interview with *Food and Wine* magazine. He's slated to be featured at their festival in Monaco this year. Let's play it up. Charge people a flat rate for food. One of his creations. Maybe a flat rate for a specialty drink."

It might work. "We won't raise the full amount, probably."

"There are other banks out there. We never sent that paperwork back to Jacob. I'll reach out to others first thing Monday." He drummed his fingers on the table.

"What is it?" The pensive look didn't suit Cathal's face.

Cathal pulled his cell phone from his pocket. "Who's going to tell Rian?"

Going out had been a mistake. Katie didn't take her to only one bar. She took her to five. Five bars from ten to almost one in the morning. Her feet ached, like usual, and she was over-wearing a strapless bra. Again, she'd tried to go out in something less revealing, but Katie refused to be her friend. Said she'd never find a guy who wanted a girl in a pair of jeans and flip flops.

It'd been all she could do to tell her that she'd snagged Brogan that way.

But Katie was out to prove a point. Ever since becoming single, Katie had replaced the pain with the fleeting excitement of meeting new people. Flirting. Kissing. Selena understood the sensation. She'd done the same thing after breaking up with Jacob. But that'd been a long time ago. And Katie was still in her early twenties. Something switched in Selena's brain last year when she took over caring for Mimi. Maturity, maybe?

Katie stood near the bathrooms with a girl, whispering, giggling, and making out, while Selena sat at the bar with a Diet Coke that tasted flat. She might love her friend, but this might, officially, be the last time she goes out with Katie.

"Well, this is my lucky night."

Simmons.

Shit.

"Is this seat taken?"

"Yes." She snapped out the words, trying to be tough.

Simmons sat down anyway. His hand immediately patted her knee, and she stood up. "Leave me alone."

The bartender, a cute, tall woman with red hair, immediately pounded on the wood top of the bar. "You okay?"

"We were just getting reacquainted," Simmons said, his eyes lingering on Selena's chest.

"I was just leaving."

He threw his head back and laughed. "You don't have your Irish bodyguards around to threaten me. But I'll have the last laugh. You know I made the owner raise the offer on the bar, right? They barely squeezed enough together for the first offer. No way they can add another five hundred thousand to it."

Five hundred thousand. The number didn't seem real. Brogan didn't have enough sitting around without having to go to the bank. She could always appeal to Jacob for them, but Brogan wouldn't want her near him again. Not on behalf of the pub.

"Did you need something to drink?" The bartender knocked on the bar again. "You."

"Kettle One. Straight up." He reached out to touch Selena's hip, but she moved two seats down.

"No touching at my bar," the bartender snapped. "She doesn't want you around, so I suggest you move along."

Selena's phone buzzed. Cathal of all people.

Came out looking for you. Which bar are you posted up?

She scanned the bar before looking back at the bartender. The redhead's eyes were still locked on Simmons. "What's the name of this place?"

"Fiona's."

She typed it into her phone. Cathal responded immediately.

Luckily, I'm right down the street.

Ha! It looked like her Irish bodyguards were still around after all.

Simmons is here.

That time, she didn't get a response.

"I'm still waiting on my Kettle One," Simmons said to the bartender.

"And I'm still waiting on you to stop bothering this lady." She pushed a strand of hair away from her face. "Can you sit there like a nice gentleman or do I need someone to throw you the hell out?"

"I've been nothing but a gentleman." He sneered at her. "I offered her a job when the place she's working closes down."

"You're the one shutting it down!"

Simmons moved down two seats, too, putting himself right beside her.

She stood. "I'm not interested."

He grabbed her by both hips, pulling her off balance in her high heels. "Stop playing me."

The bartender shouted something, but she couldn't hear it. Not with the buzzing in her ears.

She slapped Simmons again, but he smiled, his fingers gripping so hard, she began to squirm.

Her knee caught his groin.

His eyes bugged out from the impact.

And then she stumbled backward, landing on her butt. Several people helped her up as she tried to make sense of what'd happened. Had Simmons pushed her?

The bartender slapped at someone who had Simmons pinned on *top* of the bar, his legs dangling off the edge, one shoe falling to the floor from him kicking frantically.

Cathal.

She went over and tugged at Cathal's shoulder. "Cathal! Chill. God, he can't breathe."

Cathal said a string of words. Who knew what with the accent and dropping in and out of Irish. She'd be lucky if he didn't crush Simmons's windpipe with his forearm pressed into his throat.

"Cathal! Don't kill him!" She tugged harder. He released Simmons and stumbled backward with her, holding his hands up. Simmons slumped over on the floor, gasping for breath.

The bartender agilely climbed over the bar to see her customer. "Geez, man, you did about kill him." She shook her head, eyes pinned on Cathal. "Damn it. You need to calm down. I don't need this now. I just got my liquor license back."

The bouncer walked up, but the bartender waved him away. "It's done."

Selena gave her an apologetic look. "I'm sorry. It's a long

story." She stepped in front of Cathal. The pure rage on his face didn't match up with the easy-going man she knew—the one whose brothers joked about his laziness.

Twice, Cathal had gone completely crazy on Simmons. She'd have to contemplate it later.

"What happened?" Katie came over, her girl of the night right behind her. "Did Cathal go ape-shit on Simmons again? I didn't see him walk in. Either one of them."

"No, I don't guess you did." She spared Katie half a glance. "You going home or staying here?" Because, at the moment, she never wanted to set foot in another bar. Or see Simmons again.

"Staying."

"I'm going. Call me tomorrow."

Cathal's hand gripped her elbow. "I'll see you home."

The bartender stuck a hand on her hip. "Perfect! Your boyfriend nearly kills a man and off you two go without even checking on the slimy bastard who just threw up on the floor?"

Cathal stopped, eyes narrowing at the bartender in such a severe way most women might have backed away. Not this bartender. She crossed her arms, expecting an answer.

"The slimy bastard as you called him is lucky he got the brother and not the boyfriend."

"I knew it!" Katie squealed before covering her mouth. Selena ignored her. She'd try and play it off tomorrow and make sure Katie didn't say anything.

"Tell your boss they can find me at O'Keeley's Pub if they have any problems." Cathal forced Selena to move to the door and out into the warm night. "I really think Katie is not a good influence on you."

"Thanks, Dad," Selena smarted back.

His lips twitched, but he didn't smile. "Are you sober?"

"Yes. I drove. My car is—"

"I'll handle your car."

She hmphed. "Are the good looks to blame for all three of you being bossy as hell?"

"No. We were brought up to make sure a woman got home safely. You can thank our Ma for both, though."

He opened the door to his silver Mercedes. Flashy. "Are you going to tell Brogan? About Simmons?"

"Of course." He squeezed her shoulder, his voice turning softer. "Don't be surprised if he tries to see you tonight. He'll need his hands on you to know you're alright. Give him that."

"It'll be almost two by the time I get ready for bed. I figure he's been asleep for a while." He was so regimented with everything. Like a machine. A set time for everything. "Just tell him tomorrow."

"The old man goes to sleep by ten if possible because he gets up to exercise so early. He'd kill me if I didn't let him know about Simmons immediately." He scratched his jaw. "Plus, I might need to give him a heads up in case I get arrested for assault. I'll need him to come to bail my ass out of jail for avenging his girlfriend's honor."

"About that. I think Katie heard what you said. You forgot to use my official title as the *exclusive* VP of Advertising."

Cathal shrugged. "Just tell her not to say anything. I think she's a smart woman."

But Selena wouldn't mention it to Brogan. He'd run for the hills if he thought someone outside his family knew about them.

When she arrived home, Katie's sister was waiting at the door. "Sorry. I didn't think I'd be gone this long." Selena wrote her a quick check and made sure she got to her car alright before locking the apartment. No way Brogan would come by at two in the morning.

She washed her face and put on pajamas. Her body still tensed when she replayed the way Simmons yanked her, his hands on her body. She would eventually get over it.

Her phone beeped.

I'm outside.

Crap. Brogan had shown up. Selena threw back the covers and walked through the living room. She unlatched the deadbolts.

The door swung open as soon as she turned the knob. Brogan was there, hands on her, crushing her to his chest.

She patted his back. "Cathal said he'd call you."

"I'm surprised he even left the man breathing." He looked down. His expression was unreadable in the darkened living room. He'd worn a t-shirt, sweatpants, and his sneakers were untied. His hair messy. He looked like he rolled out of bed just to check on her.

"Cathal said he saw him grab you."

She shifted to the side, pushing the door closed and flipping the deadbolts. "Yes. He did."

"Why were you even near him?"

"Near him?"

"At the bar. If you'd have left...."

His gruff voice made her spine straighten. "Excuse me? How is this my fault?"

"I didn't say I thought it was."

"Yes." The anger, emotion, frustration from Simmons finally boiled over. "You did. You think I could have avoided it somehow? He sat down; I stood up. He touched me. I told him to stop and moved down the bar. The bartender told him to stop. He followed me, and I stepped away. He *grabbed* me. I slapped him, and he squeezed my hips tighter. I kneed him in his junk. Then, bam, Cathal pulled some wrestling move and almost crushed his windpipe."

Brogan growled and muttered something she didn't understand.

"I was the one who pulled Cathal off. I'm not sure your brother had any rational thought left, and Simmons isn't worth going to prison."

"That's a difference of opinion." His hands rested on her waist. "I'm sorry. I didn't mean to imply that you did anything wrong." He kissed her lips lightly. "Did he hurt you?"

"Bruised a little."

"Where." He said it in his bossy voice that usually annoyed her. Most of the time, it made her straight up mad. Honestly, right then, she didn't want some overly emotional guy that babied her. She could see how other women wouldn't appreciate his matter-of-fact nature, but that was Brogan. When things got out of control, he took over. At two in the morning, she'd let him.

She rested her hands over his, sliding them down until they set where she'd seen the fingerprints when she'd changed her clothes. "Here."

Brogan spread his hands wide and swallowed. "Can I see?"

"Do you need to?"

"Yes."

She pulled down one side of her pajama pants, enough to show him the fingerprints.

He hissed through his teeth. "I'm sorry, Selena. This is my fault."

Pulling up her pants, she shook her head. "Did you raise him to be a piece of shit? No. Neither one of us is to blame for his actions." She slipped her arms around his waist. "I just want the memory to go away."

He cupped her face. "What can I do?"

"Stay."

His hesitant expression pulled her back into the reality of their situation. She was the secret girlfriend.

"Never mind."

"No. I'll stay."

"I'm not looking for anything more between us. I don't want to be alone."

He ran the back of his hand down her cheek. "I'll need to leave before you usually wake up."

"Just nudge me when you go."

Taking him by the hand, she led him through her small apartment. It became glaringly apparent that Brogan could never survive in a place that small. The narrow hallway exaggerated his size.

He chuckled as he stood at the edge of her room. "This is what I imagined."

She looked around. Messy. She was a messy person and wouldn't try to cover it up. She crossed her arms, giving him as sexy a look as she could while wearing an old t-shirt and pair of flannel pajamas pants.

"I didn't realize a messy room would actually keep you from sleeping in my bed."

"Not much of anything would keep me from doing that with an open invitation." He flipped the light off. "Now, which side do you sleep on?"

13

Bacon.

The first thing he smelled when he opened his eyes. The second, a sweet wildflower scent that lingered in Selena's bedsheets. He rubbed a hand over his face. Had he overslept?

It was 5:00 a.m.

Her side of the bed was empty, and it disappointed him. He'd held her most of the night, not pushing anything between them physically. He'd never want that memory to come on the heels of what'd happened at the bar.

He grabbed his shirt, tugging it down and padding down the hallway to seek out the source of both delicious scents.

She stood at the stove, barefoot, muttering to the food like she needed to help it cook.

"Good morning," he said, hoping not to scare her.

She barely glanced his direction. "Oh. Good. You're up. Can you grab the plates out of that cabinet?"

He opened the cabinet she'd indicated. The kitchen was small. Smaller than the one his Ma had back home.

"How many?"

"Three." She started flipping off burners. "And it's ready. I was going to try and keep your plate warm."

"Selena," he nuzzled her neck from behind, finding the wildflowers again. "You didn't need to cook me breakfast."

She swatted at him. "I probably wouldn't have if Mimi didn't wake up twenty minutes ago, asking for food."

He straightened. "Where is she now?"

"I set her up in her room watching television. She can watch infomercials all day. At least until the soap operas come on." She pursed her lips together. "Can I leave you to plate these and I'll go grab her?"

"Sure."

Selena wiped her hands on a towel as she scurried out of the room. He stood there, dumbfounded, for a moment. The kitchen. Cooking. Selena rushing to make sure her granny got food. Surreal.

"Here she is," Selena announced.

Brogan hustled to plate the food. Rashers of bacon, eggs, and toast. He set a plate on the table, watching her granny the same way she watched him.

Uncertainty.

Did she know he'd stayed over in her granddaughter's bed? He'd been run out of a house or two in the mornings back home while still a teenager. Those memories didn't leave.

"I'm Estella Chapman." She held out her hand.

"Brogan O'Keeley. Nice to make your acquaintance." He held her thin hand lightly, aware of every bone. The only resemblance between Estella and Selena were their eyes.

Selena helped her to sit. "I'm glad to have some male company for a change. I keep asking Selena to find out if George Clooney kept any of his medical scrubs from his time on TV and might want to take over the nursing duties, but she won't."

Brogan grinned. "I'm no George Clooney, but I'm glad to have your company as well."

"What do you do, Brogan?"

Brogan paused before setting his plate down and sitting across from Estella.

Selena saved him. "He owns a restaurant."

"Oh. You should hire Selena. That boss she has now I heard is a real tyrant."

Brogan slowly turned to Selena, her nose almost shoved in the eggs on her plate. "Is he? Maybe I will have to steal her away."

Selena drank a glass of water, not coming up for air until it was empty.

He took a bite of his breakfast, enjoying her discomfort for some reason. "What else did she say about her boss?"

"Oh, the usual stuff. He won't make up his mind about her."

Selena's eyes grew round. "Mimi, I don't remember telling you that."

"She'd thought about quitting a few times."

"Quitting?" She'd quit O'Keeley's?

Selena held up her hand to keep him quiet. He laid his fork down, but she didn't seem to care about him at the moment. "When did I tell you that?"

"Oh, honey, I don't know." Estella became a little flustered. "Did you not? Sometimes things feel so fuzzy."

"Yes. I did, Mimi. I—"

"So you were going to quit?"

She cut her eyes at him. "Hold on." She took Estella's hand, patting it. "It's alright. I do remember telling you that now. Can you eat a little bit more for me?" She pointed at

Brogan's plate. "Brogan has eaten all his bacon. You love bacon."

She smiled. "I do love bacon." She picked up a piece and began to chew on it.

"I need to talk to you." He rose, not waiting for a response. Quitting? Why? He needed her in the business. They had that event to put on in a short turnaround. Cathal had mentioned two weeks. He needed her there. With him.

When he realized Selena hadn't followed him, he returned to the kitchen. She sat there, eating her eggs, unaware of the panic rolling inside him.

"Selena?"

She looked up at him. "What?"

"I asked you to come here so we could talk."

"Asked?" She set her fork down. "I don't remember you asking."

He ran a hand over his head. Why was she playing these games? "Selena, dear, will you *please* come into the living room?"

She arched an eyebrow. "No. I'm eating. I personally don't like cold eggs, and I used the last of them to make enough for the three of us."

He really was an idiot sometimes. His shoulders relaxed. He walked back to the table, dropped a kiss on the top of her head, and sat down. He wasn't used to this, considering someone else's feelings.

"Sorry," he mumbled, scooping up a forkful of eggs. They ate in silence. Estella didn't seem to notice. After Selena ate her last bite, Brogan rose and took her plate.

Her eyes shot to his. He didn't blame her for doubting his motives. He didn't have any clue how to be in a relationship.

He turned the sink on hot. But the hot water never came on. "Selena, do you not have hot water."

"Dang. It must be out. I'll go start it again, but you won't have hot water for a while."

"Have you told the apartment complex about it?"

"Oh, yeah. They jump right on things when I complain." She held up her hands as she left the room. "Sarcasm, Brogan."

He turned back to the sink, scrubbing the dishes well before setting them in the drying rack.

"She likes you, you know." Estella sat at the table, her golden eyes watching him. Her Southern accent sounded regal. "Don't let me be the reason you don't pursue a relationship with my granddaughter."

He turned the water off and dried his hands on the worn towel. He walked to Estella and squatted down in front of her. "I'm proud that she takes care of you."

"I know it's a burden. I keep hoping the insurance will pull through for her." Her eyes shined, and she glanced away.

He took her thin hands in his. "She wants to get you the best care possible. Would you like for me to help you back into the living room or your room?"

"Yes." He took a hand under her elbow, helping her rise. He turned. Selena stood in the doorway.

"I can help her."

"I got it. Where are we headed?" He followed Estella's instruction, helping back into her bed to finish getting some sleep. It was barely five thirty.

But when he returned, Selena wasn't in the living room or the kitchen. He found her in her room, sitting on the side of the bed, staring at the windowless wall.

"Are you alright?" He sat down beside her.

She leaned her head on his shoulder. "I did want to quit. I told her that when she wasn't in her current mind. I was surprised that she remembered it. Sorry I snapped at you."

He set a hand on her knee. "I really don't want you to quit."

"That's nice to hear."

"We really need you right now. Cathal has this idea to generate more income and help make up that five hundred thousand that the owner tacked onto the price. A big promotion to draw in a huge crowd."

"So my boss doesn't want me to quit. The man that slept in my bed last night doesn't have an opinion?"

That was the tricky part. He swallowed and shifted to meet her gaze. It amused him that she looked a little annoyed. His Selena was definitely not a morning person. "I enjoy seeing you at work. But if you stopped working for the restaurant, I wouldn't stop trying to pursue you. So, no. The man that's here right now still wants you, be it you work at O'Keeley's or not." It'd almost be easier if she didn't work there, but he'd keep that to himself. He relied on her too much to let his own wants or needs to get in the way.

She kissed him lightly. "I like that answer. What do you need me to do for the restaurant?" She moved to her dresser, opening a drawer and pulling out clothes.

"Plan the promotion. Make it happen. Make it a success."

She swiveled around. "What? You want me to plan a big party? I don't know how to do that."

"I mean, we'll help and everything. But we were going to feature Rian, make him the center of it."

Her lips turned up in a small smile. "Have you told him that yet?"

"Cathal drew the short straw."

She nodded and walked across the room to her bathroom, pushing the door to, but not shut. "Keep talking. I'm just changing."

He went through the ideas they'd discussed, along with a few of his own. He stretched back on her bed, not wanting to face the reality of the situation between them when they got to work.

He liked being with her, touching her when he wanted.

She opened the door. Her work shirt was tucked into tight jeans. Her hair in a ponytail. "Don't you look cozy and relaxed on my bed."

Whatever had put her in a bad mood earlier seemed gone. He grinned. "You have a very comfy bed. I'd be obliged if you invited me back to stay."

"We'll have to see when my boss lets me off. He can be a real tyrant." She sat on the bed beside him.

He reached over, gripped her by the shoulders, and dragged her across his body so he could finally kiss her good morning.

They'd kissed a few times before going to sleep the night before, but awake, lying with her, her body on his, those sweet kisses flew away.

He rolled them over, pinning her underneath him. The day would be hell. He'd go from touching her, tasting her, to acting like she didn't affect him with a single look.

She tugged his shirt. "Off," she mumbled against his lips.

"I feel like this is one-sided." But he sat back long enough to take his shirt off.

"Completely." She ran her hands over his chest before tugging him back down and kissing the hell out of him. She touched him everywhere, driving him crazy. He wanted to do the same. But that was a line he couldn't cross. Not until he figured out how to have her for good.

.   .   .

SELENA CAUGHT Katie in the bathroom before their shift started to clarify what she'd heard Cathal say about Brogan at the bar. It was a lame story about how they'd talked about going out but didn't want it to mess up their professional relationship. Basically, a bunch of crap that Katie nodded and said, 'of course,' a few times before she winked and walked out of the room.

Yeah. Katie hadn't believed a word of it.

But she didn't have time to worry about that. Now, snuggled deep into the leather sofa in Brogan's office, the challenging task of planning a big shin-dig to save the pub was her focus. The computer sat open on her lap and dozens of papers spread out across the coffee table and two other chairs.

The biggest problem she kept running into was Rian. He wouldn't return her phone calls or her texts. He was the star, according to Brogan. The star was pitching a major hissy fit at the moment.

"How's it coming?" Cathal asked as he entered the room, carrying a cup of tea in his hand. "Katie said you liked black tea."

"I do. Why is Katie still here?" It was well after four. Brogan had offered to pay for Mimi's nurse, calling it a perk of being VP of Advertising. Because they were back to that, even after the hot make-out session before leaving her apartment.

"She stopped by to give me the heads up that I'll be arrested this afternoon. Apparently, the girl she met at that bar works as a receptionist at the police station."

Selena's mouth dropped open. "No. Way. That's ridiculous!"

"Not really. I did almost kill him." He said it like he'd offered the guy a ham sandwich. Something lurked within Cathal that didn't align with his happy, flippant persona he presented to everyone. She'd seen it now. Twice.

"Almost only counts in horseshoes and hand grenades."

He laughed. "Clever. But he's still filing charges."

"I'd offer to bail you out myself, but it might take a while to get the money. Despite my new fancy title, it doesn't come with a pay raise."

"Brogan already said he'd come." He sat on the edge of the chair. "I wanted to ask you a favor. I called a lawyer friend of mine that handles these things more than I ever have. Do you mind reporting your side of what happened?"

"Not at all." She hadn't even thought about it. "What about the bartender? She saw the whole thing. She was there when he messed with me the first time. She actually told him to stop."

"I'll be sure to let my lawyer know." He pointed at the paper. "Is there something in here that is useful for the promotion? I know it's a shot in the dark, but maybe we can raise the rest of the money."

"I'm getting there. If I can get Rian to call me back so I can get some details."

"See, we tease Brogan that he's the moody one, but he has all the financial responsibility. Rian, he's moody when his art isn't going his way."

Selena took a sip of the tea. She raised an eyebrow. He'd put whiskey in her tea. "When are you moody?"

"When I'm locked away from pretty women and alcohol."

She looked at her watch. "Oh. So, in another fifty-five minutes, I'll see what Cathal looks like moody."

"Absolutely."

Brogan came into the room. Closed the door. Walked over to Selena and planted a solid kiss on her lips.

And, earlier, when they'd been in the dining room, he'd ordered her to restock the ladies' restroom with toilet paper. Back and forth they went. Forever, apparently. She pushed the negative thoughts from her mind.

Temporary. He wasn't Jacob. At least she kept telling herself that.

"Braggart," Cathal mumbled before moving the papers out of the chair for him to sit. "Give us what you've got, Selena."

Brogan sat down beside Selena. And that made her happy.

"I do have an idea. But it's pushing it. You wanted this in two weeks, so you'd have three to figure it out if you didn't get enough money, right?" She took a breath and pulled up the website. "In a few weeks, the party would coincide with an Irish festival in Atlanta. I wouldn't book it the same weekend. We wouldn't want that competition. But, it might be helpful to host yours the weekend before."

"Three weeks? You're right," Brogan said, his fingers twirling the end of her hair absently. "That is pushing it."

She looked up at him, wanting to ask another question, but he dropped another small kiss on her lips.

"I like the idea. But how do we draw people in?" Cathal pointed at her tea. "I was going to abstain, but do you mind?"

"Go ahead."

"Abstain from tea?" Brogan barely asked the question before he sighed. "I should have known you added something to it."

"We want to keep Rian's food the focus. And I think I can get in contact with a few of the food critics or bloggers or whoever to come in. Offer them free tickets for the exposure on their websites." She pulled up another website. "Now, what is trad music?"

"The traditional music you hear in Ireland." Brogan nodded toward Cathal. "He can play a fiddle if you feed him enough whiskey."

"I might have to do that. Can you do anything?"

Cathal answered. "He sings like a scuttered fish when he drinks too much whiskey."

She'd expected him to deny it, but he didn't. Something about Brogan singing horribly made her smile. He did everything else so well. "And Rian's the cook," she added.

"Oh. Rian can play the fiddle, too." Cathal downed the rest of her tea in one drink like it was a shot. "I'm just better."

"Rian would disagree." A knock at the door brought Brogan to his feet before he announced for them to enter. "Sir?" Katie peeked in. "The police just showed up. They're earlier than I told Cathal. I'm sorry."

"Don't worry about it, Katie," Brogan said. "Thank you for letting us know ahead of time. And thank your friend as well."

Two uniformed police officers appeared behind Katie. She darted out of the way.

Selena rose with Cathal. Before the men entered, she walked over to him and hugged him. "Thank you."

He ran a hand down her hair and patted her back. "It's fine. I guess I shouldn't admit it's not my first time for being arrested for fighting."

"I assumed it wasn't." She pulled back. "I'll go with Brogan to the station, file my report."

"Thanks." He turned and stood silently as the police

officers read him his rights. They walked him out, without handcuffs.

"You're going with me?" Brogan opened the desk drawer and pulled out his car keys.

"Yes."

"But, don't you think it will look odd?"

"Stop." She held up her hand. "I need to report what happened so it can go against them keeping Cathal. Take me to the station so I can help get *your* brother off these charges that he only got because he was protecting *your* VP of Advertising."

His eyes narrowed. "Are you ever going to stop calling yourself that?"

She set her hand on her hip. "Are you ever going to start calling me something else?"

"Please. Just wait and leave a few minutes after I do."

Her lips pressed together, trying to stay nice. But she couldn't. Not when it hurt every inch of her heart. "Do you want to sneak me out of the back door?"

14

B rogan watched her for a moment. "You're joking again, right?"

Selena threw her hands up. "Yes!" She grabbed her purse and fished out her car keys. "Never mind." She stormed past him. She didn't need this. Him. Not when a good man just got sent to jail because of her. Not when she was busting her ass to help his business stay open. And he won't even acknowledge that they were, at a minimum, friends and walk out together. It wasn't like she was going to straddle him in the middle of the restaurant.

Brogan didn't move to stop her, which pissed her off even more. Katie stood at the bar, looking sad as the police loaded Cathal into the back of the car parked in front of the pub.

"Thanks for giving him the heads up." Selena hugged her.

Katie pulled back. "Are you going with Mr. O'Keeley to get him out?"

"I'm going, but not with Brogan. What are you doing right now?"

She motioned to the bar. "I was going to have a beer and drown my sorrows that they put the prettiest man in Atlanta behind bars."

"Come with me. I'm going to file charges against Simmons." Selena linked arms with Katie and guided her out of the restaurant and around the edge of the building to the parking lot. She needed a friend. Someone to keep her sane.

"Selena!" Brogan's rough voice called from behind her as they approached her parked car. He hesitated when he spotted Katie. For once, she didn't care about how it made him feel. Her own feelings of being hidden under a rock, out of sight, were too strong to ignore.

She waited at the trunk of her car while Katie paused by the passenger door. "I think I missed something," Katie said. "He looks mad as hell right now."

"What?" Selena asked him, not caring about how angry he looked. She was pretty damned pissed herself.

He looked at Katie and back at her. Then back to Katie.

"Were you coming back to finish the project?" He stuck his hands in his pockets. She'd noticed him do that almost every time they were in public together. "Later?"

Selena lifted a shoulder. "I don't know. If this takes too long, then I'll see you in the morning and start where I left off."

His eyes shifted to Katie again. He looked incredibly uncomfortable. But he made the rules. This entire situation was his own fault as far as she was concerned. She wouldn't end up like her mom, taking pity on the guy and letting them drag her down again and again. Or like she'd been with Jacob like she embarrassed Brogan.

"I'll see you later," Selena finally said when he wouldn't

make a decision and walked to her door. She sat down without looking back.

Katie sat down beside her. "Damn, I hope a man looks at me that way someday."

"What way?" Angry? Annoyed? Every word that described a man like Brogan when he didn't get his way, and Selena didn't fall in line.

"Stop pretending you two aren't a thing. I won't tell anyone, but it hurts my feelings for you to lie to me." She changed the station on the radio. "He's really strict about that no dating policy, huh?"

Selena would let Katie in because she needed someone. She needed advice. "Yes. So much so that when I mentioned to him about going out somewhere, he said that wouldn't ever happen."

Katie's head snapped her direction. Selena concentrated on driving and not on the Audi following her to the police station.

"Ever? As in for-ever? What kind of relationship is that?"

Selena stopped at a red light, glancing in her rearview mirror and frowning at Brogan's scowl. "A shitty one. For both of us."

"What are you staring at? Is it Brogan?" Katie flipped the visor down and looked behind her. "It's so strange calling him that, but if my best friend is sleeping with him, then I'm at least going to use his first name with you."

"We haven't slept together."

Katie stuck her lip out in a fake pout. "He looks so miserable. Maybe you should."

"I'm not giving him pity sex. He does look miserable, though. But I feel miserable as well."

After reapplying her lipstick, Katie flipped the mirror

closed and changed the radio station again. "You have options, you know."

"Like what?"

"Well, what are your goals?"

Selena's lips quirked to the side. "You sound like my guidance counselor in high school." And that conversation had been a complete waste of time.

"I'm serious. What do you want to happen between you and Brogan? Hot, heavy, and quick. Long and sweet."

Selena pulled into the police station. "Are you talking about sex?"

"No. Get your mind out of the gutter. I'm talking about the real relationship between you two. Do you think what you have will fade away in another couple weeks or even a month or two?"

Fade away. Being with Brogan brought everything inside her alive. How could that ever fade away? The intensity had already shifted. Not lessened. Equalized a little. And she still thought about him all the time.

"I don't think it will fade."

"Alright. Can you see yourself waking up beside him for the rest of your life?"

Selena turned the car off and faced her friend. "I see myself sad if he's not with me when I think of the future." She hadn't had a serious thought about finding someone who would commit to her with Mimi's situation. Brogan had been so sweet to Mimi the other morning.

Katie tilted her head to the side. "What if you stopped seeing him right now? How long would it take for you to get over him?"

Selena blinked. Could she ever, really, get over him? She hated how he made her feel, hiding her away, but the sweet side of him kept her from leaving. None of the other men she'd dated, or even met, came close to be the kind of man she wanted. She wanted Brogan without the seesaw of emotions. *That* Brogan would never get out of her system.

"A really long time."

"Then quit."

"The restaurant?"

"Yes. Find another job."

She leaned her head back on the headrest and closed her eyes. "But I love working there."

"Do you love it more than you love Brogan?"

"No."

She snapped her fingers. "So you do love him! And you've kept me in the dark throughout this entire thing. I'd be mad at you if I weren't so happy."

Selena rolled her head to the side, watching her friend's excitement and feeling dread at the decision. "What's my other option? You said I had other options." Because acknowledging she was in love with Brogan messed with her head. She didn't have the luxury to fall in love. Not when it meant never moving in or moving forward with a relationship because of Mimi and having to give up something you love, like her job. Definitely, if it meant their current situation. Maybe she wasn't any better off than her mom. Was falling in love this easy genetic?

"There are two more options," Katie said. "The first is continuing the way you've been going."

"Yeah." She opened the door. Katie did, too. "But that sucks."

"You know your last option." Katie exited the car with Selena. "You need to break up with Brogan."

Selena turned as Brogan approached them in the parking deck.

"Oh, crap, I did it again. I'm sorry, Selena."

Brogan's eyes pinned Selena in place as he approached. "Katie, give us a minute."

"No." Selena tilted her chin up. "Katie can stay. This isn't work, Brogan. You don't get to tell her what to do."

Katie took two steps backward. "It's alright. I have a feeling this is a private conversation."

"Thank you," Brogan gritted out. He waited until she'd made it three cars away. He lowered his voice. "I see you told Katie about us."

"She overheard Cathal at the bar last night tell the bartender that he was the brother and not the *boyfriend*." She poked him in the chest. "Stop thinking I'm running around telling people things about us. And she was trying to help just now."

"By ending our relationship?"

"By pointing out that I have options if this secret arrangement bothers me, which it does."

Brogan took a breath. "I understand that. But I don't want to set some sort of double standard for the workplace."

"You already are a double standard, be it people know about us or not."

"I've been burned in the past, Selena. Lawsuits. Payouts. I can't afford to mess things up now. Not with the restaurant on the line."

She didn't know that. It made her body relax. Slightly. That still didn't apply to her. She'd never pull something like that, but she could see his worry about his employees.

"Brogan, do you like me?"

"What kind of question is that?"

Selena pushed away from her car to stand in front of him. Close enough that they would touch if either one of them moved an inch. She kicked her chin out and stared at him.

"Do you like me? Yes or no."

"Yes."

"Do you think what we have between us is different than a one-night fling?"

His body swayed as his hands gripped her shoulders. "You know it is." His rough voice and firm hands almost broke her resolve to stand up for herself. "I tried to tell you that this morning."

"Then you need to figure this out. Because if you don't want us to break up and you don't want me to quit, then you need to find a different solution. I will *not* stay hidden and in this limbo position forever." She would not end up like her mother. Or the way she'd been with Jacob. She still couldn't figure out which category this relationship fell into. The man that strung her along, coming to her when he needed something or the man that cared for her but didn't feel she was worthy enough to acknowledge.

But, damn, she sounded more confident than she felt even though her inner She-Ra cheered at her assertive demand.

His fingers cupped her chin, the pad of his thumb tracing along the bottom of her lip. "Give me just a little more time. I'll try to figure out what to do." Tilting her head up with the slightest pressure, Brogan kissed her delicately. It soothed over her frustration for the time being. Reeled her right back in like it always did.

It was dangerous loving Brogan, especially when he was still in control.

"I NEED to call the nurse if I'm going to be much longer," Selena said as she ran a hand over her hair.

Brogan shifted in the small elevator and glanced at

Cathal. His brother stood facing the doors, quiet, the same as he'd been since they left the police station. No one liked to spend a couple hours behind bars. No matter how good a reason he had. Cathal had spent more than a couple of hours in prison back in Ireland after he attacked the man who'd assaulted his girlfriend at the time.

Recently, he'd heard people saying different situations were "triggers" for them. That description fit Cathal. Men with any type of violence or aggression toward a woman triggered something deep inside.

He'd give his brother his space. Let him come back to life slowly. He always did.

"I'll call her for you," Brogan said to Selena. She'd finally started talking to him. He had a hard time not touching her, putting an arm around her shoulders and drawing her close. For that moment in the parking lot, he'd been worried more that she'd walk away from him and less about Katie finding out.

That's why he'd kissed her. Even knowing Katie watched them a few feet away. It might seem small to an outsider, but it was a big risk where the restaurant was concerned.

"You don't have to do that."

He held out his hand. "Go socialize with Cathal and Rian and let me."

"Rian? Where's he?" Selena asked, pulling out her cell phone.

"Cooking Cathal a welcome home dinner." Brogan slapped a hand on his brother's back. "His favorite."

Cathal glanced over his shoulder. "You better have a fridge stocked with beer. Any kind."

"Rian was supposed to pick that up when he brought over the lamb."

His eyebrows shot up. "He's cooking me lamb?" A stupid

grin spread across his face although his eyes stayed severely solemn. "I might have to go back to jail more often if I get Rian's lamb when I get out."

"I've never had lamb." Selena winced. "I don't know if I can eat such a cute animal."

Brogan kissed her temple. "You should try it." Keeping her in a good mood had become his priority. He refused to dwell on their fight. He hated putting her in the position of keeping their relationship a secret. It wasn't fair. He knew that.

They stepped off the elevator. Cathal made a big deal of putting his nose in the air and sniffing. "Lamb and turnip stew. And the homemade soda bread. He's gone all out."

"Rian's a chef. Doesn't he usually cook amazing food?" Selena asked.

Cathal opened the door to Brogan's apartment, pushing the door open and letting Selena walk in first before cutting off Brogan and following her.

"When he cooks, it's delicious." Cathal rubbed his hands together and turned the corner into the kitchen. "The problem is that he never cooks for us."

"That's a lie," Rian responded. "I cooked for you last year. Hi, Selena."

"Hi. It does smell delicious. My stomach doesn't seem to care about Mary's little lamb at the moment."

Brogan motioned her to a chair at the table, but she didn't notice him. Her eyes scanned over his apartment, lingering on the sitting area he had set up, similar to how it was growing up, facing an electric fireplace. He'd not considered himself sentimental until both his brothers pointed out the unconscious move. Neither one of them had wanted the furniture from their parents' home, so he'd taken it.

"This is completely different from how I imagined your apartment." She smiled a real smile that eliminated the remnants of their earlier fight. "I love it."

"I'm glad. Sit. Cathal can get you something to drink while I call the nurse for you."

"He doesn't have to do that. I can find something to drink." She took a step toward the kitchen, but Cathal held up his hand.

"No. I've been lazing about in a cell for the past couple hours. I'll get it. Then I'll take you on a tour of the apartment."

"What he means is he'll show you the balcony. It's his favorite part." Brogan took her cell phone from her outstretched hand. In a quick move, he snatched her around her waist with his other hand, pulling her close.

She gave a small yelp of surprise and then laughed. Good. He liked that sound.

He kissed her, as softly and sweetly as possible with an audience. He knew his brothers would busy themselves to give them a moment. He wanted longer than a moment with her, like their time spent at her apartment, just the two of them. Well, and her granny.

"I'll be back in a moment," he murmured and released her. That had pleased her, he could tell. She nodded her head and watched him walk into his office.

He called the contact she'd pulled up on her phone and introduced himself when Tina answered.

"Is everything alright with Selena?" she asked.

"Yes. She'll be home a little later than usual."

"What time?"

He thought for a moment. It was already seven, and dinner would be at least another hour. "Eleven?"

"Any time after ten is considered an overnight stay charge."

Overnight. He glimpsed out the office door. Selena sat with a beer in her hand, laughing at his brothers as if she'd always been a part of their group.

"Are you able to stay overnight?"

"Yes, sir. The charge is more substantial, like I said."

"That's fine. But I'll pay for it. Don't charge it to Selena."

The woman chuckled. "Alright, sir. Tell Selena that her grandmother is doing fine. She's had a good day today."

"I will. Thanks."

That'd been presumptuous of him. He'd stayed at her place before. She could stay here without any pressure. Take the second bedroom if it came down to that.

He hoped it didn't.

But she'd been right. They couldn't do this forever. He was thirty-seven. Sneaking around to see a girl seemed wrong.

Dumb, really.

But focusing on one thing at a time was productive. Resolve the issue with this business first. Then, he'd figure out the personnel issue with dating an employee. He'd figure out how to introduce it into the public view without jeopardizing his business or giving the employees the wrong impression.

Her phone chimed.

I hope you enjoyed the movie as much as I did.

From Jacob.

He blinked, trying to comprehend what that meant. Had Selena gone on a date with Jacob? Friendly? Romantic? It didn't matter. Nothing with Jacob would ever be friendly on his side. The man had watched her at dinner that night like she was his damn dessert.

I'll swing by sometime next week and pick it up. Or you can finally take me up on my offer to go to dinner.

Brogan's eyes closed with relief. So they hadn't gone on a date. His feelings for Selena had become borderline obsessive. And deep.

The thought of any other man touching her pissed him the hell off. Maybe if they didn't have to keep it a secret, it wouldn't be so bad. He wouldn't have to wonder what excuse she came up with when she didn't accept Jacob's dinner invitation.

His basic instinct was to close his arms around her, shield her from everything. He half-laughed. She'd resent him for thinking she needed it.

He walked back into the living room, spotting Selena and Cathal standing on the balcony. Rian drank a beer, his hip leaned against the counter as he scanned his phone.

"Thanks for cooking." Brogan grabbed a Guinness and poured it into a pint glass.

Rian lifted a shoulder. "No problem. He handled Simmons on behalf of all of us and managed not to kill him." He set his phone down and met Brogan's stare. "I think this will all work out. The bar. You and Selena. It feels right."

The way he phrased it meant a long, *long* future. Thinking of being without Selena brought a sour taste to his mouth. But a future? He wanted one. But for how long? Better yet. How?

"You're overthinking this, Brog." Rian pointed at the pint glass of dark liquid in Brogan's hand. "Drink. Stop analyzing everything. Stop running the numbers or whatever you're doing."

"I wasn't thinking about the bar."

"I didn't think you were. Don't screw this up with Selena.

Cathal and I both like her. A lot. She's good for you." He smiled and nodded at the window of the balcony. Selena said something to Cathal that made him throw his head back and laugh. "She's real. Down to earth. Isn't afraid to stand up to you. Apparently, she liked your condo, which only leaves her tastes questionable."

Brogan rolled his eyes. "Just because I like things that are comfortable doesn't mean I have poor taste."

"Outdated? Is that a better word?"

Brogan held up his pint. "Sentimental."

"She's also headstrong. I'm sure the two of you will come to blows from time to time if you haven't already." He tapped his phone. "She's left me four text messages and four voice mail messages. All about that promotion you want to put on."

"That we *need* to put on." Brogan shifted to watch her as she and Cathal walked back into the living room. "If the food can survive without you for a few minutes, why don't we go sit down and discuss it?"

Rian let his head drop back. It didn't matter at this point whether Rian wanted to participate or not, they needed his name to draw in a crowd. The promise of traditional Irish dishes with a gourmet edge.

Brogan sat down on his sofa, pleased that Selena sat down beside him. He passed off her phone. "Everything is fine."

"Great."

She looked at the screen and then back at him with a small shred of panic. "It's nothing like how that sounds."

Good. But he'd keep it to himself just how disconcerting it'd been a few minutes earlier. Or how much he wanted to find Jacob and tell him to stop trying to date his Selena.

She pulled up a list on her phone and waited until Rian

sat down in a wide sofa chair before asking her first question.

Brogan stayed quiet, sipping his drink, enjoying listening to the cadence of her voice. The wildflower scent that clung to her hair. The way her hand occasionally brushed over his knee. She was here, with him, not out with Jacob.

None of the women he'd dated since coming to America had brought him so much jealousy. That meant one of two things. Either those women meant far less to him than he'd realized at the time. Or, the scarier prospect.

Selena means more to him than any other woman before her.

Rian stood and left to check on dinner, Cathal making an excuse to help him while sending Brogan a curious look.

Selena shifted to face him. "You were quiet."

"Just letting you talk."

"I think that's all my questions for now. Starting tomorrow, I can work on the advertisement for it. Start pushing things out into the world and making it a reality."

"I want to pay you for this."

"Really?" She picked at something on her blue jeans, her eyes downcast. "What if I royally screw this up? Waste everyone's money and time? You might have to ask for a refund." She lifted her gaze to him.

"You won't." He pushed a strand of her hair behind her ear. "But that doesn't matter. Keep track of the time you spend doing it and send me an email every so often. I'll write you a check. You're definitely less expensive than if we hired out this job. And I know I couldn't do what you're doing. I don't have the patience for it. That's why you're the VP of Advertising."

"The invincible Brogan just admitted he couldn't do something?" Her lips pressed together. "I'm amazed."

He leaned down, kissing her along the side of her neck. "I'm not invincible," he murmured. But he felt like it with her beside him.

She tilted her head, and a sigh escaped her lips. "Your brothers are over there."

He trailed up her throat until he reached the edge of her jaw. All night. And it still wouldn't be enough time with Selena. He set his hand on her thigh as he skimmed his teeth along the edge of her ear.

"Stay. Tonight."

"I—can't. You know that."

He leaned back to see her eyes. "I asked Tina to stay. It was already an overnight charge. I'm paying."

Her golden eyes didn't blink for a moment.

"Alright, you two, dinner's done," Cathal called.

She still didn't answer but stood and walked ahead of him to the kitchen. Cathal stood at the counter, a bottle of wine open. "Would you like some?"

"Yes. Thank you. I think I'll need it." She accepted the glass of white wine and took a sip as Brogan moved past her into the kitchen. Without an answer.

15

"Dinner was fantastic." Selena passed Rian a warm, wet plate as she finished washing it. Someone else cooked, she was more than happy to clean what few dishes Rian left in the sink. "My grandmother would have enjoyed that."

"You should take her some of the leftovers." Rian smirked and hitched his thumb over his shoulder. "Don't let Cathal make off with the lot of it. He's a lazy arse in the kitchen."

"I might have to. I appreciated the night off cooking." She kept talking, trying to take her mind off the decision to stay with Brogan. And his questions about Jacob. He'd handled it better than she would've guessed. But the way his muscles tensed when she mentioned him didn't fool her.

She smiled brightly at Rian. Her distraction. "Did you always know you wanted to be a chef?"

"Yes. I think part of it was my ma pitying me. Brogan was always working. After Da died, he basically ran the farm and got another job to help pay the bills. So, Ma pulled me into the kitchen with her. When she died, I took over that aspect until we needed to move to the States."

Needed to move. She didn't miss that phrase, and she didn't think Rian had meant for her to. Selena glanced over her shoulder. "All three of you moved here at the same time?"

"We thought it for the best. Once we left, we ended up going our separate ways for a while. Cathal went to school at Georgetown. Brogan had already graduated from the University before we left, so he started random jobs here and there. Then he sent me to culinary school." Rian set the last dish in the drying rack. "We promised our ma we'd stick together. And we have for the most part. The restaurant was actually Cathal's idea after he went to an Irish pub in college and declared it to be shit."

Selena laughed along with Rian. It felt like a family. Her own had been so hit-and-miss her entire life. Her dad was gone. Her mom ran from boyfriend to boyfriend. The solidarity of them made her miss something she never knew existed outside television. But the O'Keeley's had accepted her readily.

"It's almost eleven," Cathal announced as he set his empty whiskey glass in the sink. "Good thing the restaurant won't open until one o'clock tomorrow. We all get a bit of a sleep-in. I'm gonna head home before the weather turns fierce." He put his arm around Selena's shoulders. "Come with me, darling, and I'll have Rian take you home." He kissed her temple. "I think I will officially adopt you. It's nice to have a woman in the mix."

She leaned into him. "It's nice to be part of a mix. I don't want you to go out of your way, though. I can call Katie." That was a horrible lie. She planned to stay with Brogan. If she didn't chicken out.

"Don't call her to come to get you. I can take you home." Rian picked up his keys from the counter. "If your apartment is where I think it is, you're on my way home."

"That's very nice of you." What else could she say?

"I'll take her home," Brogan said from behind her as he sat his warm hand gently on her shoulder. With a tug, her back pressed against his chest. She leaned back, his masculine energy running through her body. She wanted to close her eyes. His voice melted over her. "No worries, men."

Cathal shoved his hands in his pockets, looking a little disgruntled. "That makes absolutely no sense. The rain is moving in. You said so yourself. Why get out in it when we have to go that way?"

Selena waved her hand, hoping Cathal would drop it as she tried to ignore the way Brogan's hand skimmed along her waist to set at her hip. "Katie has my car. If she comes and gets me then I can drop her back off and won't have to worry about swapping cars tomorrow."

Cathal scoffed. "Yes. And if she's as irresponsible as she was the other night, she already needs a ride home herself."

"Katie doesn't go out every night. She's just trying to work through a break-up at the moment. She can come and get me."

Brogan's heat disappeared, and he moved to the door of his apartment and opened it. "I said I'd drive her home." His face had 'just go away' written across it, but his brothers still didn't get the point.

Rian stared at Brogan with an incredulous look. "Certainly, you trust us to get her home."

"We're your own flesh and blood, Brog," Cathal added.

Damn it. Brogan would have to deal with the consequence of it. Selena crossed her arms. "I'm staying. Here." She looked back at Cathal. "With Brogan. And both of you are making it awkward as hell right now so drop it and leave."

They both grinned. "No. I just won twenty dollars, though," Rian said. "I bet who would cave first. Cathal always goes with Brogan."

Brogan muttered something that both the men found amusing.

Selena's mouth dropped open. "You knew? And you bet?" She aimed an annoyed look Rian's direction. "And I don't know how I feel about you thinking I'd cave first."

He smiled wider and pulled her into a big hug. "I just know our brother." He turned and left, Cathal trailing right behind him.

Brogan shut the door harder than necessary, locking it. "Sorry. I tried to raise them better."

"It doesn't bother me in the least. I was trying to be discreet for you. Not me." She walked back to the kitchen and poured another glass of wine. Good God, the way he watched her about made her come unglued. She hated feeling like she wanted to flag Cathal and Rian down and take them up on their offer.

She held up the bottle of wine. "Do you want any?"

"No." His eyes held hers.

She set the bottle on the counter and picked up her glass. He shouldn't make her nervous. "You're lucky to have brothers that love you that much."

"I suppose." He walked to the sofa and sat down like this was an everyday occurrence for him. He was in command of everything in his life. He expected her to follow him, just like at her apartment.

She was the only one that was on the verge of going crazy!

Things needed to change. She couldn't spend the night

wondering what he was thinking. Waiting on him to make a move. Hoping she didn't move too fast. He probably had the entire night planned out. Selena couldn't say for certain how far she planned to go with him. Sleeping with Brogan was at the top of her list, but not at the risk that he'd squash on her heart come Monday morning when he treated her like a generic employee again.

She didn't want special treatment besides a smile and kiss 'hello' in the morning. After taking a sip of her wine, she left the glass in the kitchen. She wanted to be in control, too. Of herself. Of the situation.

"I take it there's supposed to be a big storm coming?" She walked to the sofa. A perfectly lovely sofa cushion sat empty beside Brogan.

She sat in his lap.

He blinked and then recovered, his hand holding her thigh, so she didn't fall on the floor. "Yes. There is. I assume this means you decided to stay? All night?"

She kissed him hard on the mouth. "What gave you that idea?"

"Just so we're clear—"

Selena pressed a finger over his lips. "Be quiet. I'm a big girl. You won't pressure me into anything I don't want to do. I don't want to talk about it again."

"You're bossy."

"You are, too."

He trailed his fingertips up and down her leg. She was about to be a puddle of goop if he did that much longer. Brogan's hands *anywhere* turned her to mush.

She leaned closer, nipping once at his bottom lip before sinking slow and deep into the kiss she'd wanted all night.

A loud knock at the door broke them apart. His head fell back before he shifted her to the side and stood up.

"I left my cell phone," Cathal called. "I swear if you're already naked, I'll be so damn proud—"

Brogan yanked open the door. "Do you mind? I have neighbors."

Cathal brushed past him. "Sorry, love," he said to Selena who still sat on the sofa. "I forgot my phone." He picked it up off the counter and waved to Brogan. "Carry on."

Brogan slammed the door harder that time, muttered, again, and then stalked back to the living room.

Selena rose. He'd expect to start back where they left off.

She met him in the middle of the floor. Brogan needed a little chaos in his life. And right then, riding high on the happiness of feeling part of a happy family for once in her life, she was the one to give it to him.

"We could—" He didn't finish his sentence as her lips found his. If the kiss on the couch had been rated by intensity, she'd have given it a three. This was a six. She rose up on her toes, trying to get closer. She'd promised she'd stay the night. Yet his hands stayed PG. Hers had already slipped under his shirt. The brief experience of his skin when he'd stayed at her apartment had left a lasting impression.

Now, she wanted to memorize every inch of his amazing chest. Hard chiseled muscles. The one she felt every day smoothing down his tie.

Another knock at the door made her moan in frustration this time.

"That jammy bastard had better be glad I don't—" He opened the door, and Cathal stood there with a dopey grin on his face.

"Sorry. Left the lamb." He moved into the apartment, sent Selena a wink, and then turned to leave. "Carry on."

"I'm not answering this door again," Brogan growled.

"I didn't expect you to answer the first two times."

Brogan closed the door and locked every lock imaginable.

Some more of Cathal's magic she assumed, pushing Brogan's buttons.

He started to pull her back to him. But she had a different plan. Keep him off-kilter. Not in control. She was in charge.

She stepped back, just out of his reach. "Where's your bedroom?"

His brows drew down sharply. Nothing but sweet, polite concern in his expression. Because *that* was what she wanted to see.

"Selena...."

She rolled her eyes and pulled her t-shirt over her head, tossing it to the far chair. The bra was plain, same as before, but judging by his sharp intake of breath and the way his eyes locked with hers, it didn't matter.

"I'll find it myself."

After a few more phrases she didn't understand, he took long, confident steps and yanked her to his body. His mouth crashed into hers, smothering her squeal of excitement. His mouth ravaged hers, the same way he'd done before. Primal. When he lost his edge of control, they both won.

Her feet left the floor, and she wrapped her legs around his waist.

This was happening. He'd finally given her the level ten kiss she wanted.

Another knock sounded at the door.

His lips trailed down her throat.

"Bedroom, Brogan."

Never breaking contact, he moved across the living room and away from the front door.

. . .

SELENA'S HANDS and lips almost made Brogan forget he was nearly forty and should handle the situation with a little more finesse. He'd dreamed about carrying her to his bedroom, laying her down on his bed. And here she was, in nothing more than her plain bra and a pair of blue jeans. Both of which were sexier than lace lingerie when they were on her beautiful body.

"Please tell me you have a condom," she muttered against his neck. She'd already stripped him of his shirt before they fell onto the bed together. He'd managed to get off both shoes and one sock without breaking the spell and having to lean down. There just was no nice way to take off a pair of socks.

Brogan reached to his nightstand and flipped one out. He'd checked for one himself partway through dinner.

Selena shifted and unbuttoned her jeans.

Brogan set his hand over hers, keeping her from going farther. "Wait, I—"

"Stop second-guessing me, Brogan. Please. I want to do this." She nodded her head as if to make the point clear.

The reassurance was helpful to hear, but that wasn't his hesitancy. He rested his forehead to hers, a combination of still being completely aroused and trying not to laugh. It was an odd feeling.

"I was going to tell you to wait." He leaned back and pushed her hands away. Slowly, he unzipped her blue jeans. "Because I have done nothing but watch you swish your tail around the bar in these tight jeans, and I'm going to enjoy finally getting the chance to take them off you."

"I don't swish," she said with a fake pout. Her down-turned lips shifted into a sexy grin as Brogan pulled the pants down her thighs. He still had flashbacks of her pulling down her pants far enough to tuck in her shirt in his office that one time.

And now his hands were on those hips.

His lips found hers again, and he suddenly wished he had accepted the second glass of wine. Maybe then he wouldn't feel the emotions battering into him like the waves in the Atlantic Ocean as he stripped off the rest of their clothing.

He kissed along the curve of her neck and down to the swell of her breast. His hands shook, and he was thankful for the darkness. That was the last thing he needed to explain right then. To himself or to Selena.

The wildflower scent that drove him crazy lingered along her skin. Every inch he discovered, touched, tore away the last barrier he'd built around his heart. The final distrust of her melted away.

Because Selena was different.

Her back arched against his chest, her fingers interlaced with his and pinned above her head.

He squeezed his eyes shut against a surge of protectiveness. The woman gave him more than he could ever return. But he'd protect her. It didn't matter what happened, what they became, he'd make sure this woman was protected.

A blur of emotions swirled through Brogan's system, and he swore their hearts were beating at the same rapid pace as he entered her.

Her back arched again, their bodies pressing together.

He held still a brief second, the sudden awareness of how much his life had changed since he left Ireland completely overwhelming him. He never assumed he'd find someone like Selena.

He never knew someone so perfect for him existed.

"Brogan," she mumbled, her hands skimming along his back.

He wished he could tell her, swear that he'd be there for her, but that was for another time. For now, he'd try to show her.

16

T he loud crack of thunder caused them to jump from a deep sleep. Selena curled up closer to Brogan, her head nuzzled on his chest, just under his chin.

He wrapped his arms around her tighter with a flash of lightning and, after a moment, a crash of thunder. "Are you scared?" He pressed a kiss to the top of her head, enjoying the memory of their night together.

Her finger trailed along his stomach, where the sheet rested low. "No. It's nice, though. Not having to listen to it alone. Mimi is probably up." Her voice didn't hold any trace of sleepiness, although she spoke in whispers with him.

"Tina has her." He kissed her hair again and rested his cheek on its softness.

"I know." She took a deep breath, her exhale trickling warm air across his chest. "This is the first night in a year I've been away from her."

Simultaneously, thunder boomed and lightning struck again. This time, they both jumped and then lightly laughed. "It'll move through soon." Without the lightning, his room filled with complete darkness. He felt her head angle upward. Her lips pressed against his jaw. It seemed impossible that it would ever get old. Selena. In his arms. In the dark. In his bed.

He took a guarded breath. Why wasn't the rest of life this comfortable with her?

Her lips found his. The flash of heat from before was gone, replaced with nothing more than raw emotions. A little painful it hit so deep within him. With every press of his lips and touch of his tongue, he spelled out how much he cared, hoping she knew.

Last night reaffirmed the same revelation he'd experienced with their first kiss. Something inside him clicked into place. Now, the darkness helped. He didn't have to face the questions in her eyes. Expectations. Responsibility.

In the dark, it was only their two souls. Calling it love, when they were both so open, seemed trivial.

What pulled them closer together was something deeper than he knew the words to describe. So he didn't try. He'd give what he had and take what she offered. Cherish this one moment and figure out how to live with or without it in the morning.

SELENA SCANNED through her email on her phone as Brogan drove her back to her apartment to change before work. "I don't think Cathal went to sleep last night. The last few of these emails came in at six this morning. He didn't have to do all this for me."

Fifteen emails. All with information about possible ways to afford Mimi's stay at a nursing facility. She'd barely touched on the topic at dinner, both brothers asking how her grandmother was doing. Or granny, as they called her.

And now, it seems she had a friend willing to help. Focusing on Cathal's emails prevented her from analyzing her night with Brogan. His hand rested on her knee as he drove. What they had between them felt real and significant. He seemed to feel the same way if she read his signals right. Would it last or would he revert back to the aloof man that only acknowledged them behind closed doors?

She was royally screwed at this point. Love. It might not make sense to anyone else, but she loved her grouchy boss. The tender way he'd held her, loved her, put a hitch in her breath when he turned his brooding gaze her way.

"What else does he have to do?" Brogan asked.

She cleared her throat from the emotion. "Does he have another job? He is a lawyer, right?" She'd tried to figure out how to get Mimi into a home, but, everywhere she looked, either said her insurance wouldn't pay for it at this stage, or she had to pay out of pocket. Each time it frustrated her. In a matter of hours, Cathal had a game plan.

"He works for a firm when they need him. Odds and ends from what he says. You should let him help you with this."

She wrinkled her nose and stared out the window as they pulled into her rundown apartment complex. "I hate asking for help."

He parked and turned off the car. "Think of it this way." He tucked her hair behind her ear, pulling her face close and kissing her lightly. "You're helping me with the restaurant, so he can help you with your granny."

Exactly how a family treated one another. The emotion from before welled up inside. But she couldn't tell him she loved him. There were too many hurdles between them.

"I still feel bad he spent his entire night researching this, but I will accept his help. As much as I hate asking for help, there's no denying I haven't been successful on my own." She pushed open the car door as Tina appeared in the doorway with a frantic look on her face.

Selena bolted up the steps, taking two at a time. "What's wrong?"

"She fell. Just now. I called for an ambulance—"

Selena pushed past her, Brogan right behind her. Mimi laid on the floor beside her bed.

Selena dropped to her knees beside her, immediately reaching for her head, cradling it in her hands.

Tina's voice shook when she spoke. "She called for me and then I heard her fall. She won't let me touch her now." Tina sobbed out something else and left the room.

"Mimi?"

Mimi pulled away, crying, looking between Brogan and Selena with wide, scared eyes. It'd happened this way before. She'd snap back into another time when something scared her. Hurt her.

"Let me help you up," Selena tried again, but Mimi lashed out at her with her other hand. The hand she clutched to her chest looked odd, her wrist hanging unusually.

Selena's stomach rolled. "I think she's broken her wrist."

"Aye." Brogan's hands gripped Selena's shoulders and pulled her up and to the side. Without giving her grandmother an option, Brogan squatted down and picked her up, setting her gently back on the bed even though Mimi got one or two strong slaps in with her good hand across his cheek and forehead.

Mimi held her wrist and rolled toward the wall, muffled sobs shaking her frail shoulders.

Brogan brought his arms around Selena, and only then did she feel the tears on her cheeks. Helplessly, she stared at the small form of her grandmother. This was why she needed the facility, with nurses who knew what to do. All she did was guess at what to do for Mimi.

The paramedics arrived, and Brogan left the cramped bedroom to give them space to work. They took Mimi's vitals and decided she did need to have a doctor look at her wrist. She still wasn't in her right frame of mind and flat out denied even knowing Selena. The paramedics asked Selena to meet them at the hospital in an attempt to keep Mimi calm,

Again, she was useless.

Selena watched the ambulance drive out of the apartment complex. She needed a shower. Change of clothes. Then she'd go by and pick Mimi up from the hospital.

"Have some coffee." Brogan passed her a mug. "I watched how you made yours this morning."

Their morning together seemed so long ago. Brogan's sweetness eased her heart a little. "Thank you. I'll have to call for another nurse. Tina said she couldn't stay any longer today."

"You don't have to come to work." He leaned against the railing near the stairs that led to the parking lot. The early morning sunlight caused Brogan's eyes to glow a beautiful shade of cobalt blue.

Last night had changed things. An uncomfortable buzz of emotion swirled in her chest. She didn't think it was regret. Brogan hadn't shied away from her. Hadn't become distant. But he looked just as confused as she felt. Mimi's episode had catapulted them both straight back to reality.

"I might not have a choice but to take off today without a nurse. I'll need to go to the hospital in a couple of minutes and wait there until I can bring her home. I have the company's laptop. I'll work on the party once I get her settled."

"You don't—"

She held up her hand. "Please. It will give me something to take my mind off this," she said as she motioned around her apartment complex. She didn't want to live like this, scrapping every penny possible to take care of Mimi and never getting ahead.

Never giving Mimi everything she needed.

Never having a future with Brogan.

She wiped away the tears that'd formed again before they could fall. She hated crying. Between her love for Brogan leaving her exposed and the fear for her grandmother, Selena hated the overwhelming feelings threatening to bury her whole.

Brogan pushed off the railing and took a step to stand in front of her. He held onto her shoulders, his hands as firm as his tone of voice. "I know you can handle your granny, but let Cathal help, Selena."

She swallowed over the lump in her throat. Her grandmother's situation was only partly to blame for the tears, burning her eyes. At the moment, she would focus on that situation and ignore her love for Brogan and the big mess that came along with that.

"I feel selfish. Like I shouldn't want all this freedom."

"You are not selfish." He cupped her cheek, his thumb brushing along her temple. "You're human." He pressed his lips to hers, gliding her into a slow, steady kiss. He cared. That much she'd wrap around her for the moment. He was the only stable thing to hold onto, if only for a fleeting minute.

He lifted his head, a small smile on his lips. "Go grab a

shower, as you mentioned. I'll drop you by Katie's to get your car as I go into work."

She kissed him one more time. Last night had been wonderful. Back to reality today.

BROGAN STOOD up as Selena walked into his office. She closed the door and sagged back against it. "Since when is coming to work supposed to feel like a vacation?"

He'd not seen her for two days. Two miserable days that'd left him feeling empty and disoriented. In an attempt to gain back a shred of control, he'd oversaw her shift personally, staying on the floor and running the dining room.

And his employees hated it.

But she was here now, and that made the chaos in his mind settle. Her dark circles, lightly visible underneath her makeup, matched her tired expression.

He walked to her, debating on how to greet her. Because once they opened the door and their workday began, he was back to square one with treating her like an employee. The way she absolutely hated.

He'd considered calling a big meeting with his staff and laying out the relationship for them, but that seemed partly ridiculous since he didn't even know what to call her. Girlfriend?

That sounded dumb at his age.

"Another bad night?" he asked.

She lifted a shoulder, watching him with her golden eyes. "Not *as* bad. The medicine helped her sleep. Tina is finally recovered from the trauma." She reached out and tugged his tie, bring him closer. "Kiss me and make this a good morning."

He'd do that every morning if he had any clue on how to get to that point with her. She shifted their kiss immediately. He wouldn't push her. Not with everything going on in her life.

But Selena's teeth grazed his lower lip, her hands gripping his shoulders, and, suddenly, there wasn't anything else in the world but the two of them.

It was his only explanation for reaching around her and locking the door.

She pulled his tie off his shirt and began to unbutton. "I want skin," she mumbled against his lips.

He gripped her hips tighter. "Do I get skin, too?"

"As much as you want," she said as she untucked his undershirt.

"No. Not that much." He slid his hands underneath the back of her shirt, caressing the smooth skin of her lower back. "Once I start, I won't stop."

"I probably won't say 'no' Brogan," she said, a smile in her voice.

"I'm not a teenager that runs around with a condom in their wallet, Selena," he replied.

Her hands slowed down then. "Oh," was the small, disappointed sounding sigh that escaped her lips.

He laughed. "Sorry. I'll be sure to carry one around for us."

"No. It's probably for the better." She leaned back, resting her head against the door as her hands ran along the length of his chest. "That would make it hard to concentrate on work. All I'd do is try and figure out a way to be alone with you."

If she stayed with him, they'd have that time in the morning together *before* they had to work. Which, unfortunately, they had to do.

"Speaking of that, you know we still have to keep all of this low key. It won't be forever, but please, let's get past the purchase of the property." He smoothed her hair away from her face.

Her eyes narrowed and lips pursed. "How is it so easy for you to flip it on and off?"

He leaned his body into hers, pinning her against the door. "Don't think for one moment that I want this any less than you do. Cathal's livelihood. Rian's name. Everything I've worked for since coming here might be erased if I don't handle this right. Like O'Keeley's never existed." He kissed her with a rough edge he tried to control and ended it just as quickly. "But I want you, Selena. All I'm asking for is a couple more weeks."

He shifted, needing air.

Space.

Selena drove him to lose his mind. The thought of her walking away because he couldn't figure out how to be her boyfriend and her boss, made his head pound. And scared him. For the first time, he found someone worth giving up everything. But O'Keeley's wasn't his to give up.

She began to button his shirt, keeping her eyes averted. "I'll play this your way, for now, Brogan." As she buttoned the top button, she lifted her eyes to meet his gaze.

How had he ever thought anything between them would be simple?

Because based on the way she watched him, she was about to make his life hell. And damn it if he wouldn't enjoy every second of it.

"So what are the rules?" She lifted an eyebrow. "I assume I don't get to slap your ass as you walk by."

He laughed, enjoying the playful way she ran her finger

along the edge of his neck. "No. You don't. Nothing that lets anyone know we see each other outside this office."

"Then I'll only slap your ass while we're in the office." She held up a finger. "With the door closed, obviously."

"You're going to make this difficult, aren't you?"

"Did you have any doubt? I don't like feeling hidden like I'm not good enough for you."

How could she ever think that? Jacob, the snake, had put that insecurity into her mind. "You're more than I deserve, Selena." He slipped his tie behind his neck and tied it for a second time that morning.

She straightened his tie. "The only hope you have right now is that I'll sneak you into my bedroom after curfew."

He smiled at her small laugh and dipped his head, bringing their mouths in line. "As long as that can happen tonight—"

Brogan's head snapped up when a knock sounded at the door.

"Mr. O'Keeley? Sir?"

"Crap! It's Trey," Selena whispered. "What's he doing here this early?"

Brogan shifted to the side. If he were behind closed doors with Selena, this early in the morning, it wouldn't take someone even as dense as Trey to figure things out.

"Go. Hide in the bathroom."

Her mouth fell open. "You're actually *hiding* me now!"

"Yes." He tucked in his shirt.

Selena shook her head with a mischievous look in her eyes that Brogan didn't trust. "Payback will be hell, Brogan."

"I accept my punishment. Just go!" He waited for her to shut the bathroom door before opening the office door. "Trey? You're here early."

"Yeah. I'd hoped to talk to either you or Selena. I saw her car out back. It's about my shift."

Her car. The staff knew she was working extra hours in the morning, but no one except the kitchen staff had actually arrived while she was still in his office. And never behind closed doors.

And now Trey had nearly caught them.

Brogan pretended to look confused and stepped to the doorway, glancing around the dining room. "I don't know where she's run off to. Maybe the supply closet?"

Trey shrugged. "It's alright. I didn't know if I could get moved back to the second shift? My little brother just started a new job, and we have to share my car." He scratched the back of his head, looking down at his shoes.

Brogan never remembered being that awkward in life. But, by the time he was fourteen, he was a significant source of income for his two younger siblings and mother. That didn't give him a chance to be awkward.

"Was there something else, Trey?"

"Yeah." After a long pause, he finally made eye contact again. "Can I get some advice?"

Brogan crossed his arms. The longer Selena stayed in the bathroom, the worse the revenge. "What is it?"

"It's about a girl I like. Katie thought I should ask your brother's opinion."

"What's your question?"

"Good morning!" Cathal appeared in the doorway. "Am I interrupting?"

Everyone was interrupting.

"Trey, this is my brother. I assume he's the one Katie suggested you consult with your woman problems."

Cathal patted Trey on the shoulder. "You need to learn that women are the sources of all problems and all solutions. The solutions are much more fun, though. Speaking of women problems...." He raised his eyebrows, subtly glancing around the office. "How's yours coming along?"

Trey grinned, goofy and gap-toothed. "Wow. We all have women problems. Cool. Like male bonding."

"It's not *cool*. And I do have things to do," Brogan shot back.

Cathal glanced down. Selena's purse set on the bench just inside the door to the office. His eyes trailed around again, lingering on the closed bathroom door.

"Trey. I'm afraid Brogan can hardly handle his own problems at the moment. And by the looks of things, they are mounting by the second. I'll pour us both a coffee, and you can spill." Cathal sent Trey toward the bar and then stuck his head back inside the office. "Please tell me you didn't hide her in the bathroom."

The bathroom door swung open. Selena. Her eyes darker than usual and aimed his way in a death glare.

"Now who's the idiot?"

He shoved Cathal back out of his office but kept the door open.

She held up her hand when he started to speak. "Payback, Brogan." Her shoulder skimmed his chest as she moved past him.

She paused at his office door, taking a brief look in the direction of the bar before she hurried across to the employee break room.

Watching her all day and then waiting until he could sneak into her apartment later to touch her would be payback. God knew what she had in store for him.

17

How did he not get the message that she wanted him to leave? Selena had listened to Jacob ramble on for the past thirty-two minutes and fifteen seconds based on the digital clock on the bank sign just down the street from her apartment complex. It was also eighty-one degrees outside, and they offered a 1.2% interest rate on their car loans. It meant something that the billboard at the bank was more interesting than her ex-boyfriend's ramblings.

She wouldn't invite him inside. Her Southern grandmother, asleep, would have killed her. She'd expect Selena to invite him in, offer him something to drink and eat, and then listen to him with polite attention.

But she didn't care. She wouldn't have answered the door at all except she'd expected Brogan. But, knowing her behind-the-scenes boyfriend, he'd take one look at Jacob, throw a very quiet fit about her talking to him, and not even venture near her apartment until he left.

Help them all if the banker knew they were dating.

"I think the next movie we watch we should do it

together." Jacob smiled and pulled out his phone. "What are you doing next weekend?"

She *almost* replied with 'I'm washing my hair' but managed to hold it in. "I don't know yet. I don't know if I'm working."

"Do you work every day of the week?"

"If I'm lucky."

He reached out and set his hand on her shoulder. "I hate seeing you so run down like this."

"Then you can leave any time," Brogan's voice replied from the end of the balcony.

She snapped her head his direction. When had he shown up? And he'd actually shown himself in front of Jacob.

"I didn't expect you here." Jacob didn't drop his hand. Instead, as if they had something more between them, Jacob moved closer, his hand sliding to rest at the back of her neck.

Selena was trapped. Her next step would put her back inside her apartment. Her position, standing firm at the threshold, was the last line of defense before etiquette forced her to offer him a glass of sweet tea.

Brogan's eyes lingered on Jacob's hand. "Is this a bad time, Selena?"

"No."

"Yes," Jacob answered. "We were setting up our plans for next weekend."

He crossed his arms, towering over both of them. "Ah. You've a mind to go on a date next weekend?"

"Yes."

"No." Selena glanced at Jacob, suddenly hating how close he stood. His eyes were soft. His chin was weak. He wasn't Brogan. "I'm not dating you again, Jacob. I've told you that at least a dozen times."

"But—"

"No." She moved his hand from her shoulder. "Look. I've tried to be friends with you, but I can't do that if you're only here because you expect us to pick up where we left off."

Jacob motioned toward her apartment. "Things could have worked out so differently for you, for both of us, if we'd pushed through our problems back then. You're not the least bit curious if we still have a connection?"

"No." She might not live the life he did, nice car, an apartment with hot water, but she busted her ass to get what she'd had. Brogan had never once offered to swoop in, pay for everything, insinuate that she wouldn't live in this lifestyle if she *allowed* him to take care of her.

She appreciated that. Pride meant something to her.

"I guess there's nothing left to say." Jacob stuffed his hands in his pockets and turned. His eyes held Brogan's for a brief moment before he scuffed his feet all the way down the stairs. Extra slow. As if he gave her time to change her mind.

They waited, in silence, until his car drove out of the apartment complex.

"Look, I know you have a dozen questions."

He stalked toward her, his expression unreadable.

She backed up and into her apartment. Was he mad? If she'd shown up at his condo with a woman touching him, acting as though they were "together" she'd be mad as hell right then.

He closed the door. "No." He held her chin lightly with his fingers. "That idiot is the last person I want to think about."

His kiss confirmed why he'd come to her apartment.

"Tell me now if you don't want this," he murmured against her lips. "Turn me away. Kick me out."

"But I promised you revenge." She tugged at the t-shirt he'd worn, pulling it over his head as they stumbled down the narrow hall.

"Is this it?" He did the same to her, dropping her shirt in the floor of her room as he shut the door behind him.

She shook her head. "No. I was going to tease you. Make you want me." She smiled against his lips. "Wear something short and skimpy and make you drool. And hold out as long as I could."

"And now?" His fingers nimbly unfastened the button of her jeans. "Are you turning me away?"

"Jacob bored me so bad I'd rather have the action over revenge at the moment."

"Thank the Lord," he murmured against her neck as her head dropped back. He trailed his lips back up and kissed her again.

He tasted of whiskey, a flavor she knew now from Cathal. "Why were you drinking?" Because he didn't.

"Because I changed my mind two dozen times about coming over here." He pushed her jeans down her hips.

She laughed as she began to unfasten his jeans. "If you have to drink to sleep with me, we might need to reevaluate this entire situation."

"I had one drink, and it was to get out of my own damn way and stop coming up with excuses not to drive over here. Believe me," he said, softly cupping her cheek. The blue of his eyes felt magical for a moment. His voice was rough when he spoke. "I plan to memorize every, single, inch of your body tonight."

Revenge would definitely have to wait.

. . .

CATHAL WORKED alongside Selena at Brogan's dining room table. He sipped on his beer and typed into a laptop that cost more than three months of Selena's rent.

And he tried to find a solution to her grandmother's situation.

He filled out form after form on her behalf. It'd take her an entire week to do as many as he had. But he understood things like that. She didn't have the patience to figure it out. Instead, Selena threw everything she had into planning the party.

Part of her was nervous that after declining Jacob's offer, that he'd somehow pull back on the loan. But the loan was still firmly in place, if Jacob had even tried.

Five hundred thousand was their new goal.

Selena priced out the tickets and estimated the number of people who would come. It gave her a general guess at a profit from the bar.

The best she came up with was three hundred and fifty thousand. They were still short.

She sat back and rubbed her temples.

Brogan's strong hands rested on her shoulders, kneading them. "Oh my God, this might be better than sex," she mumbled.

Cathal's head whipped up. "A neck massage? I obviously need to have a long talk with my brother."

She giggled at his mock outrage. "Your brother is just fine."

"Fine?" Brogan repeated in a low voice.

She looked up to where he stood behind her, trying not to laugh at his offended expression.

"I still think I should have that talk," Cathal murmured. "Maybe pull in Rian for a tutorial."

Selena slapped playfully at Cathal's shoulder. "Don't bother. It's not like I'm going to get into details with you."

Cathal lifted a shoulder. "Sure, then. I'll just sweet talk them from Katie."

"Katie?" Brogan's horrified voice made both Cathal and Selena grin. "Surely, you didn't—"

"No, I didn't." She sighed and set her interlaced hands on the table in front of her. "Brogan is amazing, and all I do is try to plan a way for us to be together again. Satisfied?"

Cathal cut his eyes at Brogan. "I'm not the one that needs to leave here satisfied."

Brogan dropped a kiss on the top of her head. "I apologize for my brother. Both of them, as Rian would be no better if he were here. How far are you into the planning?"

"With all my estimates, at most the pub can make about three hundred and fifty." There. She'd said it. She didn't want to disappoint him. They'd done so much to help her and, she'd failed to construct an event to raise the full amount. But she couldn't charge any more for the tickets. She'd consulted three experts, foodies who went to these types of events often, and none of them thought it'd be successful with a higher ticket price. Not with their level of clients, working-class that wanted a pint and good food.

Brogan's eyes shifted to Cathal, and he shook his head. "You know I don't want to do that."

"Do what?" She asked.

Cathal shrugged. "Our property back in Ireland can be put up for collateral. We can pull the rest of the money from there. We already have approval from the bank."

"Seriously? That would be great."

"No. It wouldn't. It puts everything we have at risk." Brogan crossed his arms.

Selena stood up, rubbing her hands up and down his

biceps, trying to ease his tension. She'd never owned anything in her life except her small car. Taking that kind of risk would be nerve-racking. But she believed in them.

"Trust yourself and your brothers. If they're both in agreement, then that would mean you're outvoted in the matter." She smiled as his frown deepened. "All three of you own the bar. All three of you own the property. Not just you."

"I listen to them—"

She kissed him hard and quick, shutting him up. "That's not what I meant. You're not responsible for everything. The world doesn't rest on your shoulders. You aren't the only one responsible if you don't save O'Keeleys. Or if you do lose the land." She slipped into his arms when he finally uncrossed them. "You weren't responsible for Simmons."

His arms tightened.

"Or for Crissy."

"How did you know about that?"

"The internet." She glanced over her shoulder. "And a little bit from your brother."

Cathal shrunk lower behind the screen of his computer as Brogan glared at him.

She understood Brogan and his reservations better after that. But it'd confused her as well. Surely he didn't think of her the same way, that she was playing him for money. That was worse than him hiding her away, for whatever the reason may be.

"You've got to let them share some of the responsibility." She rose on her toes and kissed him. "Let me share it with you. I'm planning this thing. If it goes bad—"

"It won't be your fault."

She smiled. "Hell yes, it will be. At least partly." And she didn't have a dime to her name to help with the purchase of the building.

But she supported him because she loved him. He might not be ready to hear that yet, but she did. And pulling it back now seemed impossible.

As long as he didn't continue to hide her in bathrooms.

She kissed him again. "I need to get going. We have an early morning. The tickets to the event go on sale tomorrow. I have a few radio spots I've snagged."

Brogan shifted away. "I'm not going on the radio."

"No." She pointed at Cathal. "But he is."

"Me?" His crooked smile only added to his wicked charm. "You think I'd be good on the radio?"

"I think you'll be the best one to do it. Rian is barely participating as it is. Brogan, bless his heart, would sound like a public service announcement. You, on the other hand, have a personality."

"I'm not sure I like your description of me," Brogan said. "I have a personality."

Yes. He did have a great personality. But getting him naked and coercing it out of him was out of the question. The longer he stared at her, the more she realized his thoughts had headed in the exact same direction.

"Can I come by later?" he asked.

"Please, do." And she left, without giving in and dragging him to his glorious king-sized bed.

"WHERE'S OUR FAMOUS CHEF?" Selena snapped out the question as she walked into Brogan's office. "I have a food blogger here to interview him now. Two more a little later."

She'd worn a suit.

A nice, tidy suit with closed-toe high heels.

"You look very nice," he said. That stopped her.

She smoothed a hand down her skirt. "It's Katie's."

"You don't own a suit?" The question popped out before he realized it'd been a mistake. Her pleased expression closed off.

"No. I don't."

"I didn't mean it as anything more than a simple question."

Her shoulders relaxed—a little. "I know. I'm just peeved at your brother. Any idea when the famous O'Keeley will make an entrance?"

"He'll be here. He just got in this morning from Ireland."

"Can you call him and find out when? I'd like to let the blogger know." She tapped her foot. Her eyes narrowed. "Why are you smiling?"

"Because you're such a fierce little thing and for once your annoyance isn't aimed my direction."

"Oh. Just wait. I'm sure you'll get the next round. Stop grinning like that."

He waved her forward. "Then come here and let me apologize for my brother's tardiness."

Surprise popped into her expression. He had to get past his issues. He'd taken what she'd said to heart the night before. Not everything was his responsibility. It still felt that way. Logically, he knew otherwise.

She scooted around his desk to stand in front of him.

He kissed her, refusing to give in to the urge to unwrap her, layer by layer, out of the suit. Her hips bumped against his desk. If he took another step, he'd set her on top, step between her legs, and then, help him, he'd use that one condom he'd finally shoved in his wallet.

He unbuttoned the top button of her dress shirt. And then a second one.

"Someone's feeling frisky this morning," she mumbled before grazing her teeth along his earlobe.

Cats were frisky. Brogan needed his hands on Selena. His Selena.

The second, third, and fourth button unfastened.

"Ms. Chapman?"

Selena broke the kiss at the sound of her name called from the dining room. Heavy footsteps headed the direction of the office.

"Shit!" She looked around, her hands gripping her shirt together.

"Down," he murmured.

She complied before shooting him a murderous look.

Yes.

He'd just hidden her underneath his desk.

That wouldn't end well.

Not a half-second later, a large man with a long beard appeared in the doorway. "I was looking for Selena Chapman."

"I'm Brogan O'Keeley."

The man moved into the room. Selena was officially stuck.

"Nice to meet you. I'm Kenneth. I run a food blog. I was hoping to interview Rian O'Keeley."

"I'm here." Rian rushed into the room. "Sorry, just flew in from Ireland."

"For real?" Kenneth shook his hand. A little bit of awe covered the man's face. "Were you doing a food event?"

"No. Checking on some family business." He tilted his head toward Brogan. "That I got resolved. So, everything is set."

That meant he got the money off the land. He swallowed

down that rush of anxiety and tried to focus on what Selena said.

Brogan sat down at his desk, giving him a clear view of her as she finished buttoning her shirt. She sat back on her knees, her arms crossed, glaring at him. Her bottom lip poked out a little bit farther than normal. He had a sudden urge to kiss her.

"Where is Selena?" Rian asked.

Brogan drummed his fingers on the desk. "She's currently, um, detained. She'll be along shortly if you'd like to go to the upstairs dining room and start the interview."

Rian's lips pressed into a firm line, and he knocked on Brogan's desk. "Good luck."

Brogan needed more than good luck. Rian and the blogger left the room, and Brogan pushed back in his chair to let Selena up. He offered her his hand, but she ignored it.

"Brogan O'Keeley," she began, sounding just like his Ma when she was angry.

He moved back, holding up his hands, trying to contain his laugh. "I panicked." He walked over to the door, closing it and locking the doorknob. He didn't need anyone to walk in on this.

"I'm finally going to ask this. Are you ashamed of me?"

He blinked at the left turn her comment took. "Ashamed? No. Never. I've told you that before." He was a lucky bastard such a wonderful woman like Selena would give him so many chances. He wanted to tell everyone about her. But some things were harder to overcome.

"Do. Not. Hide. Me. Again." She crossed her arms. "Because I think it will be pretty easy to keep my hands to myself after that stunt. Under a damn desk? Seriously!" She shouted and started to brush past him. He reached for her arm, stopping her with a soft touch. "I don't think you want to do that right now."

"Selena—"

"No." She turned toward him, pushing him back with one finger on his chest until his back hit the door to his office. "You don't get to touch me. Not until I tell you to."

"Is this your revenge?" He smiled, thinking it was payback for a split second until she didn't respond, her golden eyes serious. Now he was worried.

She yanked his head down to hers, kissing him with a wildness that rocked him deeply. He gripped her hips, but her hands encircled his wrists, slamming them back against the door harder than he'd give her credit for.

"I told you not to touch me."

"But—"

She kissed him again. His hands fisted into tight balls. It was torture then. She apparently didn't have the same rules seeing as she explored his body as much as she pleased.

He moved his hand but caught himself at the last second. She obviously wanted to prove something. She wanted control.

He was as easily frustrated as a toddler by not getting to touch her in return.

She broke the kiss, both of them breathing heavily.

"Can I touch you now?"

"No."

"That wasn't very nice of you," he said. His voice sounded strained.

"Neither is someone feeling embarrassed of you."

She'd mentioned Jacob had done that to her. Hidden her away. The mental image of her kissing him that way sent Brogan over the edge before he had a chance to pull in his anger.

"Is this how you handled Jacob, too?"

Her mouth dropped open, her eyes wide.

Wrong thing to say. Again.

She pointed her finger at him. "I accepted the way Jacob treated me. I believed, for a very long time, that I wasn't as worthy as other women. Kissing you and not letting you touch me was the revenge I thought of when you hid me in the bathroom. It was the only thing I could think to do to get that feeling out of my system. Off my skin. To feel something other than inadequacy. To feel in control and know you really wanted me."

"I'm sorry. I didn't realize...."

She crossed her arms. "Move. I want to leave."

He thought about forcing her to keep talking. But he couldn't do it now. Rian and the blogger expected her for the interview.

"We're going to talk about this later."

She lifted a shoulder. "We'll see."

He nodded and shifted to the side. She left his office. He closed his eyes and leaned against the wall. Two and a half more weeks until he'd rewrite every employment contract if necessary to give himself and Selena permission to be together.

18

She hated staying mad at Brogan. Her reaction to the entire thing had been a little extreme. Selena thought back to the way his lips had twisted each time he'd glanced under the desk.

He hadn't panicked like someone might find out.

He'd thought it was funny. The man who didn't have hardly a sense of humor had thought the entire thing was funny. And she'd gone and blown it up like a big fight. Thrown Jacob in his face, knowing it'd get a rise out of him.

She'd tried to play it off, but even that had turned into a fight.

"Darling," Cathal began, walking toward her and turning every female's head as he passed by the tables. The bartender raised her eyebrows at Selena before shifting away. A waitress picking up the drinks shared a look with the bartender. Great. So no one was allowed to know about her and Brogan, but Cathal made it seem as though they had some type of relationship.

But it also gave her a small reality check. The other employees *would* talk. It would make things a double standard for Brogan like he'd worried about. She understood his rationale, knew why he wanted to handle one thing at a time. First, the purchase of the bar and then the employment issue.

They had one day until the big party. She could make it.

"Hi, Cathal." She took the papers from him as he held them out. "What's this?"

"The approval for your financial assistance for the assisted living facility."

She scanned the paper, the words a blur. He'd done it? He'd gotten Mimi into the facility. She threw her arms around his neck. "Thank you! You're amazing!"

She pulled back and kissed his cheek.

The man blushed a little.

"Is there a reason you're kissing my brother?" Brogan's deep voice made her jump.

"Absolutely," she said and spun around in the bar stool to face him. She passed off the paperwork. "She got in."

It was a surreal feeling. Brogan reaching down and giving her a hug, in front of people. It wasn't a sexual hug or followed by a kiss, but it was something. He pulled back, smiling. His hand lingered on her shoulder.

Half the waitstaff on the second shift didn't know her other than working on the restaurant's promotion. Several of them watched their interaction. And it bothered her. Mostly because he'd made such a big deal about it and made her acutely aware of the attention.

"When can she move in?"

Cathal, elbow resting casually on the worn bar top, pointed at the paper. "I scheduled it for the beginning of next week to let us get past this weekend."

"And I don't need to sign anything?"

"No. Not after you gave me Power of Attorney. I'm acting on her behalf."

Brogan squeezed his brother's shoulder. "Good going."

That praise seemed to light up Cathal from the inside. "Thanks." He clapped his hands together. "I'm headed out to celebrate. I hope you allow me to help you move her there."

"Me, too," Brogan said. "If Rian doesn't run away after the party Saturday, count him in as well. I can set up the moving truck." He dropped his voice. "If that's alright?"

"Yes. I would appreciate that." She took a deep breath. "I'm sorry. About earlier."

"No, I am."

Cathal cleared his throat. "Good. Glad we have that settled," he said loud enough they both turned to look at him. And then both simultaneously realized they very much had an audience watching them.

Selena rose and closed her laptop. She'd double-checked her to-do list for Saturday twice already. "I'm headed out."

"Have a good night." Cathal nudged Brogan in the opposite direction. "Let's go."

"But—" He started to say something. The bartender watched the scene with both eyes and ears wide open. "Same time?"

Did he mean later that night or tomorrow morning? "Yes." She'd just have to find out later.

Katie's options from before shifted through her mind as she drove home. Maybe quitting wouldn't be the worst thing in the world. At least if she quit as a waitress, she wouldn't be involved in the gossip. She wouldn't even have to work at the restaurant. Running the advertising side of their business had turned into a full-time job.

Plus she could always find another part-time job.

She did love her job, but now she knew more than ever that she loved Brogan more.

RIAN MUTTERED UNDER his breath at the six chefs in his kitchen, working through the dishes the pub might offer at the charity event. Brogan stopped trying to understand what he said. He muttered in so many damn languages, it was a waste of time. Brogan understood Gaelic, but not enough to speak it. He knew certain words in French, could manage Italian.

At last count, Rian was fluent in Gaelic, French, Italian, Spanish, and Dutch. And maybe Mandarin. He could do his two favorite things in the world. The first was to communicate with other chefs. The second was to communicate with women. He didn't parade them around like Cathal, but he suspected his brother could charm just about any woman he wanted.

He didn't talk about it, and Brogan knew he'd never settle down, not after his last marriage ended in devastation.

Brogan leaned against the wall watching and letting the aromas from the dishes whet his appetite. The first dish they offered was fish, turbot he thought, with leeks, clam and mussel and cabbage. Everyone who'd tried it had loved it. Even Katie, who, according to Selena, lived on Taco Bell, cleaned her plate at their initial tasting.

The second dish the group had fought over. Rian initially wanted to do a Guinea hen. Both Selena and Katie had shot that one down, not that Katie was in the decision-making process, but she did represent their clientele. Cathal was disappointed with that outcome that hen was only second to the lamb in his book.

Fillet of beef was their second option. He kept it to himself that the dish included a small sample foie gras. Selena didn't seem like she'd enjoy knowing she ate duck liver.

"How are the cooks doing with the menu?"

Rian shook his head.

Brogan's nerves shot up the longer he remained silent.

"Great. They got it down. Saturday night should run without a hitch."

Brogan shifted to face his brother. "Then why do you sound annoyed?"

"Because that means we're actually going through with this." His lips pressed into a thin line, and he crossed his arms. "I could always come back here. You know, back to Atlanta when the rest of the world became too chaotic. The menu at O'Keeley's is my creation, but it was never labeled as that. The restaurant is hardly mentioned at all in the articles that are written when I do competitions or demonstrations. I suppose it might have helped us, but I enjoy the anonymity. The break in the pace."

"I get it. I appreciate you putting yourself out there for us. Selena said the ticket sales have been incredible. She's even sold drink tickets for the specialty drink."

"Who let Cathal be in charge of that? I told him what we were having, and he picked a damn whiskey cocktail."

Brogan chuckled. "He had to have some input. And we all knew it'd be whiskey he picked." Cathal had proved himself much more involved when asked. He showed up when told. He handled the loan at the bank and Selena's granny's situation. He still didn't have day-to-day responsibility, but Brogan might find a place for him.

"Irish Redhead. He picked the drink in honor of the

bartender at the bar where he assaulted Simmons. Her testimony cleared his name."

"Is that all he did for her?" Rian's question was met with another round of laughter.

"I think so. He tried to talk to her, but she didn't want anything to do with him."

Rian's shocked expression matched his own when he'd found out. "I didn't know such a woman existed. We should take her picture and hang it on the wall as it's equal to a picture of the Loch Ness Monster, I'd wager. A fictional character that you don't think it exists until you see it with your own eyes."

"He was very disappointed, I think. I suspect he'll try again in a couple of weeks. You'd think he'd just move on to the next pretty face, but the way she declined his date intrigued him. She told him that she didn't date violent men."

"Violent," Rian said the word, probably hating it the same way Brogan did. "He does have that tendency, but only in very peculiar situations. And until your Selena found herself in trouble, he'd not acted out since we left Ireland. Fifteen years. I wouldn't call that a violent man."

Brogan had thanked Cathal dozens of times, but he'd brushed it off and thanked Brogan in return for saving his arse both times he'd found himself behind bars for the same situation.

He patted Rian's shoulder. "Tomorrow will go smoothly. Selena has driven herself short of mad with all her lists. I even have a list."

"Oh, she gave me a list to cover my lists," Rian said.

"See. After the event, you can crawl back into trudging around Europe, discovering new food and women. Your happy place." Because Rian hated staying stationary. Always had. The middle O'Keeley needed to ramble around the world. It kept him from remembering his own painful past.

"I thought about sticking around this fall. Traveling the United States." He motioned to the ten cooks prepping the food for tomorrow. "Seeing how I can improve this. I realize I prepare traditional Irish dishes, but they aren't always authentic. Americans aren't used to some of those flavors. I'd like to find a way to merge our culture with theirs. A new fusion. Something unique."

"Have at it. I'll be here, buying a multi-million-dollar piece of property, leaving every night hoping a pretty golden-haired woman lets me see her one more time."

Rian nodded. "Yes. Try not to mess that up, please. Cathal and I both like her. She's not afraid to call you on your bullshit."

"Thanks. You should put that in her birthday card come November. It's a nice sentiment."

They both chuckled, and Brogan left Rian to his preparations. He had just enough time to find that pretty woman and sneak a few kisses before things in the restaurant became too busy.

19

S elena shouted at the bartender over the music. "I need my order." He shrugged and pointed at the back up of tickets. She moved behind the bar to help. The fundraiser had turned into near chaos. Controlled chaos. And if she were in charge completely, she'd have already fired this bartender, whoever he was.

"Miss?"

Selena glanced over her shoulder. An elegant woman, with blunt-cut bangs, raised a finger to get her attention. She reminded her of a model, like Naomi Campbell. Only prettier, if that was even possible.

"Just one second." She set the two beers on her tray and grabbed the ice scooper, tossing some ice into the martini glass to let it chill. "Yes. What can I get you?"

The model held up a menu, pointing at Rian's name. "Is Rian actually here?" Her accent was French, maybe. Hard to tell over the noise.

"Yes. He'll be around soon so everyone can meet him. Did you get to try his food?"

Her red lips pressed together. "Not tonight, no."

That was an odd way to answer. "Do you know him?"

"Yes. I'd hoped to see him. He's a hard man to track down. Do you know where he is? I had something important to discuss with him. I'm an old friend." After a beat, she added, "It's *really* important."

Intrigued that such a woman would want to see the quiet, aloof Rian, Selena motioned her toward Brogan's office. "Why don't you follow me?" She flagged down Katie to deliver the drinks to the table before slipping through the crowd to the office door. The tall, gorgeous model made Selena feel more like a high school kid in jeans and sneakers than a woman. This was the type of woman she pictured Rian dating. The tabloids always had him linked with some leggy model. A beautiful woman like the one following her, with amazing ebony skin, fit that description.

Selena reached for the doorknob.

"You don't need to knock?"

Since Selena wanted to say, "I'm sorta sleeping with the boss," but she couldn't, she simply smiled and opened the door.

"Hey—" Brogan started before he schooled his features. "Who's this?"

Cathal and Rian were leaned over Brogan's desk looking at something and laughing. All three wore dark suits, looking impossibly handsome.

"I never got your name." Selena turned back to the woman, but her attention was latched onto Rian. Sexual heat, mixed with anger filled her expression. Selena suddenly regretted barging into the office without getting more information. Rian didn't need anything stressing him out.

"Camille Dufour."

Rian's head snapped up. The smile dropped from his face as it'd never existed.

Brogan's eyes snagged Selena's. "Was there a reason she needed to see Rian?"

Selena shrugged, hating the way Brogan looked at her like a mean school teacher. "I didn't ask." She held up her hand when he opened his mouth. "Don't start with me. I'm about to pull both you and Cathal to come to work the bar. The new guy you have back there has a backlog the size of Stone Mountain. The woman said she wanted to see Rian, and, well, look at her."

"Camille," Rian said, moving from around the desk. Slowly. Warily. Like she might strike. The heat in her eyes had disappeared completely. Now, only anger sizzled.

The backlog of drinks could wait. This was better than Mimi's soap operas.

"What are you doing here?" he asked. Did his voice crack like a ten-year-old kid?

Camille crossed her arms, giving him a sexy as hell smile that looked more like she wanted to tear his head off instead of his clothes. She rattled something off in French.

Rian's face turned instantly red.

Cathal's mouth dropped open. "Shit," he mumbled.

Rian stuttered, in several languages, not making much sense for a moment. "I did not!" he shouted.

Camille started yelling at Rian again, louder. Her red fingernails, matching her red lips, flashed under the overhead light as she spoke with her hands as much as with her quick words.

Brogan held his hand up, and she stopped, turning an icy glare his direction. Good thing nothing intimidated Brogan.

"He needs to go out into the crowd for a few minutes.

You can wait here and resume your tongue lashing then or schedule another day to assault him verbally, but right now is not that time." Brogan barely glanced at Rian. "Go. Outside with Cathal." He looked to Selena. "You, too." Brogan was in charge and let everyone in the room feel it. At that moment, Selena appreciated him figuring out what to do. Getting out her phone and trying to translate whatever insults Camille threw at Rian was her next plan of action.

And if Rian wouldn't tell her, she'd squeeze it out of Cathal.

Camille cocked her head to the side. "Do you boss everyone around, sir?"

"Yes," all three of them said in unison.

Brogan rolled his eyes and buttoned his suit. "I run a business. *This* business. Now, you are welcome to wait at the bar. I'll charge your drinks to Rian's tab since this appears to be his fault."

A flash of humor lit her brown eyes. "I hope his pockets are as big as his ego."

Selena patted her on the back, guiding her out into the hallway and toward the bar. "Bigger. Have at it."

Outside, Rian waited across the hall in the employee break room. "Are you hiding?" Cathal asked.

"No." He stepped outside. "But I don't have to worry about her running up a tab. She doesn't drink anything but wine. Most of the types she likes we don't stock."

"How closely did you know that woman?" Brogan asked.

Cathal chuckled. "Close enough for her to, well, call him a few creative phrases, compare him to the size of a snail for slinking out of her room in the middle of the night, after stealing her recipe for something that sounded like a sex position. Clafoutis?" Cathal imitated Camille. Even Brogan laughed.

"You didn't!" Selena's eyes shot to Rian. Not the quiet, reserved one.

He was flustered. "I would never steal a recipe!"

Selena gave him a shove that didn't even move the big guy. "No, you goofball. I meant about sleeping with her and then sneaking out. That's so trashy. It's something I'd expect Cathal to do."

Cathal nodded in complete agreement.

"It would have been very awkward. I assure you. Neither one of us planned to end up in bed together."

"How long ago was this?" Brogan asked, his hand skimmed along Selena's lower back, resting on her hip, out of sight of the crowd. The intimacy of the touch caused her breath to hitch.

"About six months."

The amusement faded from Brogan's face. "In Europe or here?"

"Paris."

Brogan had that disapproving dad-look down pat.

Selena gave Rian a small nudge in the direction of the dining room. "Go mingle. For all you know, Katie will hit on your lady and make her a better offer than you ever could."

Brogan's frown deepened. "I don't know if I approve of Katie hitting on customers."

"It was a joke," Selena said, following Rian. The night was a success, and not even Brogan's hot and cold emotions could bring her down. "Cathal. Bar."

"You created a monster," she heard Cathal mutter.

Yes. Being the boss was a little addicting.

"WE'RE GOING TO MAKE IT." Selena clapped her hands and

spun in a circle in the middle of Brogan's office. Her excitement was contagious, and Brogan smiled.

All three of the O'Keeleys watched her. "Do you think she nipped the whiskey when we weren't looking?" Rian asked.

Brogan watched her face shift from joy to annoyance, glad for once it was aimed at Rian.

She planted her hands on her hips. "No. I just pulled the real-time numbers from the cash registers. We'll make it for the money you need to buy the building." She launched herself at Brogan.

He caught her, tight around her waist. "That's great!"

Cathal and Rian had equally broad grins. "I'll be right back." Cathal left.

Selena's lips pressed against the spot right behind Brogan's ear. Yes. He wanted to haul her back to his apartment and keep her there for the rest of the weekend, but they still had a restaurant full of guests. Except Rian's angry one-night stand had exited the building already. She'd told him off two more times before stomping out of O'Keeley's and not looking back. Apparently, she needed some closure.

It was close to midnight, and none of their patrons looked as though they were close to leaving. They'd decided to have a two o'clock last call, with closing by two thirty. Hopefully.

"Here we are." Cathal returned with the best bottle of whiskey in the house.

"You're paying for that," Brogan said.

Selena pulled away, leaving him feeling empty. He wasn't sure exactly what he'd do about her yet. But if they'd resolved the building issue, he'd figure it out first thing after they signed the paperwork purchasing it. She might laugh at the title, but with the success of the event, he might have to make her VP of Advertising and something much more permanent.

"A toast," Cathal announced.

"Keep it clean," Brogan muttered. He'd not subject Selena to some of Cathal's more creative toasts.

"Here's to women's kisses, and to whiskey, amber clear; not as sweet as a woman's kiss, but a damn sight more sincere."

Selena giggled and tossed back the whiskey. She pointed at Cathal and then Rian. "Now. It's time to give them a taste of who you are."

"I already cooked for everyone in the dining room, Selena," Rian said. He shoved his hands in his pockets and looked disgruntled. "And talked to them."

"Brogan said you played the fiddle."

Rian shot an accusatory look to Brogan. But Cathal interjected first. "It'll be fun, Rian."

"The band you have out there might not be up to it." Rian's lips twisted to the side in a smirk. Oh, he would definitely play. Brogan did not doubt that.

Selena waved them toward the sofa. "Brogan brought these over."

"They were taking up space in my closet anyway." Brogan had to hunt to find them in his apartment. "Go play. And play well. Selena said she's putting it on the internet."

They grabbed their cases and opened them, both grinning like two kids. He'd missed being with his brothers this way. Selena had brought that back to them.

He and Selena needed more time together, but the more he thought about it, the more he agreed with his brother. They both wanted to adopt Selena into the family.

He could make that a permanent addition by asking her

to be his wife. The idea didn't scare him. Not nearly as much as losing her did. He'd screwed up so many times with her. Why hadn't she upped and walked out already?

After they'd tuned their fiddles, Brogan followed them out of the office. People watched them as they passed. Mostly, their attention stayed on Rian. They'd turned him into a sort of celebrity for the evening. A title that Rian hated when around his family. He didn't seem to mind being the world-renowned chef on the covers of magazines, but when he was at his restaurant, when he was back to being nothing but Rian O'Keeley, he wanted nothing to do with the fame. He'd said it himself earlier.

But now, watching him climb onto the makeshift stage with Cathal beside him, Rian looked happy. Truly happy.

Brogan crossed his arms and took a deep breath. His ma would be proud.

The band cut their current song short. The din of the restaurant took over the brief silence. "Should I make some type of announcement?" Selena asked as she stepped up beside him.

Brogan shifted her in front of him slightly, wished he could wrap his arms around her shoulders. "No. Cathal will get their attention."

She leaned back, her shoulder brushing against his chest. "You sound excited."

He shrugged. "I guess I am. It's been a while since I heard them play."

Cathal pulled up the fiddle and started. No preamble. Nothing announcing him. The music in the room drew the crowd's attention.

Swallowtail Jig.

He knew it well. It was the first song Cathal learned to play. Light. Quick. Lively.

Rian took over partway through, causing the crowd to cheer. Yes. Their chef could fiddle and do it well.

The band sat there, stunned.

Cathal spoke to the band for a moment before turning back to Rian.

Brogan barked out a laugh.

Selena seemed amused. "What is it?"

"Dueling fiddles. Cathal treats it like a real duel." Their ma used to shout about how hard he'd end up playing, losing all his technique. He'd even ended up smacking Rian upside the head once with his bow.

They started slow, building up until everyone in the restaurant clapped along. He took Selena's hand and twirled her in a circle, bringing her back in close. Laughing. He loved her laugh.

Dozens of people started to dance to the music with them. They shifted from song to song, the band picking up and looking as though they enjoyed the change in routine.

At close to one in the morning, Cathal and Rian finally gave up.

Trevor walked up with an arm draped over the shoulders of a waitress named Susie. They both looked tired but excited. Trevor pointed at Selena, standing to the side. "So, Mr. O'Keeley, I thought, since you and Selena are a thing that it meant I could finally let everyone know that I'm dating Sue. I mean—" Trevor grinned and pointed at Selena, "You two look good together."

A hot flush ran over Brogan's skin. This was what he'd avoided. Since the lawsuit that almost destroyed everything, he'd vowed to never put the business, his brothers, at risk again.

Seeing Trevor, holding Susie's hand, brought it all back again.

Brogan opened his mouth to respond, to tell Trevor it wasn't any of his business, but Trevor kept right on making everything worse.

"It's pretty cool, you know. You have a woman now." He grinned and held up Susie's hand. "I have a girlfriend. Maybe we can double date."

Brogan scanned the room, his mind racing. Five other employees stood near the bar, watching him and Selena.

Selena appeared oblivious. She finished clapping along with the crowd and turned back toward him. She reached out, but he stepped to the side. They still couldn't do this. Not yet.

He'd let his guard down long enough. Enjoyed himself when he shouldn't.

The happiness in her eyes disappeared. She shook her head. "I can't believe it. You have your money, Brogan."

"I just need to figure it out," he said as low as he could with the crowd. He tilted his head toward Trevor. "I can't put everything at risk. After the sale is finalized—"

"You keep saying that."

"Selena, just wait a second."

She held her hands up, eyes shining. "I can't do this anymore."

Rian and Cathal walked up, their laughter dying on their lips as they spotted Selena, almost in tears. He hated that he was the cause of them. Hated that he had a damn audience.

"What the hell did you do now?" Rian shouted. The outburst so unlike Rian, that Brogan stared at him a moment before he could think of an answer.

But he didn't get a chance. Selena ran a rough hand through her hair. "I...I don't know what I'm going to do, but I can't do this any longer. I'm done. I quit. It makes it easier, right? To walk away from what I love—"

"Wait!" His world tilted for a moment, his stomach dropping. She's done with him?

In that one moment, he didn't give a shit about his restaurant. He only cared about Selena.

He opened his mouth to say that.

"It's too late, Brogan. There's no other way." She crossed her arms, looking determined.

The pain was too much. He swallowed, his throat feeling like dust. Control. He needed to control his emotions and reaction.

She wanted him to forget his obligation to his family. Rian and Cathal were his responsibility, be it she understood that or not. He couldn't put their future, livelihoods at risk. If she couldn't wait any longer for him to figure it out the right way, then there might not be a way.

"Fine. You're right." Brogan shook his head. "We can't do this any longer. You obviously don't understand how the business world works. Not everything can be done your way when you want it done. Some things are more important."

No! His heart screamed at him that he was wrong. Selena was the most important thing.

But she took a step back like she'd been struck.

Rian rounded on him, his hand landing hard on Brogan's shoulder. "What the hell is your problem?"

Selena shoved Rian to the side, her expression a level beyond angry. Furious. What the hell did she have to be mad about? She'd broken up with him.

They were done. Her decision.

"I quit my job, Brogan," she said, saying each word slowly like he was dumb. "I didn't break-up with you."

That stomach-dropping feeling hit him again.

"But I am now."

Then she left. Walked out the front door of this

restaurant. Didn't get her purse. Didn't worry about finding a ride. Nothing. Just left him there, reeling in his stupidity.

He'd ruined it himself. Trying to protect his brothers had made him destroy his relationship with the only woman he'd ever loved.

"You don't deserve her." Rian turned and walked out the front door after her.

Cathal took strong, deep breaths.

Brogan deserved it. He knew that before Cathal hit him.

His jaw made an awful cracking sound but popped back in with the first attempt. Cathal had left by the time Brogan blinked a few times to see straight.

That had silenced the crowd. He didn't make any sort of apology. He didn't bother to answer whatever question Trevor had asked. He turned and walked back into his office, gently closing the door.

He'd tried to save the restaurant and ended up losing everyone in the process. His brothers would eventually come around. They'd give him hell for a long while.

But Selena.

He hadn't meant what he'd said. It'd made sense in his head, what he'd tried to get across. It didn't matter. In the end, he'd lashed back out at her and had succeeded in pushing her away.

Ruining everything.

He grabbed the bottle of Jameson and walked to the sofa. A $200 bottle of whiskey should dull some of the pain of his life going to shit in less than five minutes.

20

Selena blinked, disoriented. She sat up, not recognizing the room. Where the hell was she? The room was devoid of anything personal. A hotel? It wasn't Katie's house. It didn't smell like incense and French toast. For some reason, Katie's house always smelled like French toast.

She slipped from the bed. Her eyes felt fat and puffy when she touched them. Then she remembered.

The crying. A lot of crying.

That brought last night into focus. Rian. She was at Rian's apartment. She'd started crying on the way home and remembered falling asleep. God, did he carry her inside? How embarrassing.

She crept out of the room. Rian stood in his kitchen, shirtless and in a pair of dark gray sweatpants. A tattoo across his back surprised her. It looked like words curling across his back like a snake.

"Good morning," she said.

He snapped his head around. "Good morning to you." He held up the frying pan. "Eggs?"

"Sure. Thanks."

The other bedroom door opened. Cathal came out also wearing sweatpants but with a shirt with *I Love NYC* across the front. Odd.

His hand was wrapped.

"What happened? I don't remember you hurting your hand last night."

His lips were grim. "I hurt it on a hard-headed man."

"You hit Brogan?" A pang of guilt flooded her.

"Yes." He didn't pause but walked into the kitchen and pulled out two bottles of water from Rian's fridge, one for himself and one for her. "How are you feeling?"

"Like I'm all cried out for the next decade. I'm sorry. You guys really didn't have to do all this for me." If she had the ability, she'd start up the waterworks again judging by the sickening feeling still hovering in her chest. "Have you talked to him since we left the restaurant?"

Both men looked at each other and then back at her. "I'm glad you didn't wake up last night. He stopped by."

"Where was I?"

"Asleep in my bed." Rian seemed amused. "A fact that peeved him to put it mildly. He took a cab after downing most of a bottle of that rare Jameson whiskey. For a man his size, you'd think he could hold his liquor a little better."

"The sot," Cathal mumbled.

Selena walked across the almost empty condo. Calling him a minimalist was the best description. White marble floors. Black furniture. Chrome kitchen.

She sat on a stool at the counter while Rian plated her eggs. She didn't know what to expect, but from such a renowned chef, her eggs looked plain.

"Did he say anything?" She didn't know what he might say. He'd already declared his business more important than her. Her nose began to tingle, signaling the threat of more tears. Sometimes it sucked to be a woman.

"He said plenty. After forcing us to listen to a few rounds of *Whiskey in a Jar*. I swear that man can't sing to save his life." Cathal sat down beside her. "He's hurting pretty bad about now, I suspect." He set his arm around her shoulders. "You have to know he didn't mean what he said."

She wanted to, really, but it hit too close to home. She wasn't worth it. He'd said the words be it he knew what she'd meant when she quit or not. He made her worst nightmare come to life.

"He thought them. The fact he would have said them or not doesn't change." She looked at Cathal. "If you didn't think he meant them, then why did you hit him?"

"Oh, he deserved the hit for saying it, be it he made up shit at the moment or not. You scared the daylights out of him when he thought you were breaking things off. Could you not see that? He can school his features, throw on a mask that lets him boss everyone around. But when you said that to him—" Cathal shook his head and took a long drink of water.

Rian leaned on the counter. His eyes weren't blue like his brothers'. They were an interesting shade of hazel, blue-green. "What Cathal and I both noticed last night was the last time Brogan let that much emotion breakthrough was when Ma passed. You have his heart, Selena, be it the man knows his own mind or not."

She pushed the eggs around on her plate. "So, you both think I should forgive him? Pretend he didn't mean it when he told me I wasn't worth more than his business to him?"

"Hell no!" Cathal shook his head. "That man needs to come to you. He has some serious groveling to do to get his head out of his own arse. He will."

Her lips twitched, wanting to smile, which seemed wrong. "I think the saying is to get his foot out of his mouth."

"No. The man can't see daylight he's so concerned about himself."

"I think he's concerned for you. And Rian. He feels this huge responsibility to make sure you are both successful." And she'd never do anything to jeopardize it. That's why she'd quit. Because she wanted Brogan more than that job.

And he'd chosen his job.

His brothers.

He'd chosen his brothers over her. She squeezed her eyes shut. Why didn't she see that last night? Brogan hadn't chosen the restaurant or even himself. She looked at the two men staring at her. She twisted the cap of her water bottle off. "I know he misunderstood what I meant, but I think he meant what he said."

"No—" They both spoke at the same time.

She held up her hand. "He said that some things were more important. To him, you two are his world. He might have lashed out with how he said it, but the meaning was true. In that one moment, forced to make a decision, he chose you both over me."

They looked at each other as it dawned on them, too. Rian shook his head. "I'm sorry. We would have never put that choice to him. We keep telling him he doesn't have to take care of us, but he won't listen."

The pain lessened. Granted, she wasn't happy at what he'd said, but she understood it. Because she knew what was in his heart. He'd been the provider for so long. That was a hard habit to break.

"I don't blame him."

Cathal opened his mouth to speak, but she covered his hand with her own.

"No. I've been involved with your brother for what, a month give or take? A month. I love him, although I've never had the opportunity to tell him. But, when it comes down to it, it's been a month. In Brogan's thinking, when he thought he had to choose between running the business the way he thought best and taking care of you both, or me, he chose you. I wouldn't want to be with a man that'd turn his back on his family after seeing a woman for a month."

Rian ran a hand over his face. "You're a jewel, Selena. I swear, if Brogan screws this up with you, I'll kill him myself. You have to be the sweetest woman I've had the pleasure of meeting, aside from my own Ma. You deserve someone far better than my brother, but if you'll have him, I'll know he's taken care of."

She'd found a family she didn't even realize she'd craved. She leaned over and hugged Cathal before rising and hugging Rian.

"I'm afraid I'm not that sweet. I still owe him some serious payback for hiding me in the bathroom."

21

B rogan waited outside Selena's apartment. They were scheduled to move her granny at eight. It was nearly seven now. He'd been awake since three, running over in his mind what he'd say to her. His brothers had been quiet about any thoughts Selena had shared the day before when they'd driven her home from Rian's condo.

He touched his bruised jaw. It still hurt to chew.

He'd chosen the restaurant, his family, over her. And in the process had shattered his own heart. It'd taken that thought of losing her to realize how much he truly loved her. And he did. Completely. The words he'd spoken shamed him. Family, the people he loved, were more important than anything. Rian. Cathal.

And Selena.

Until he'd lost her, he was blind to realize she'd made her way onto that list.

The door opened, and he rose from the top step. Selena stood there, dressed in short exercise shorts and a small tank top.

"Hi," he said. He cleared his throat. "Good morning."

"What are you doing here?" She crossed her arms. His mind blanked for a moment. He was here to apologize, beg her to forgive him, and all he could think about was her lack of clothing.

"I wanted to talk before my brothers showed up."

"I don't have time to talk to you today. I have a lot going on." She raised her arms over her head, reminding him of a cat stretching and revealing her stomach. "Besides, it's early."

He swallowed and focused on her face. Not her body. "Selena, I'm sorry about Saturday."

Her lips pursed together. She took a second before answering, pulling her hair into a high ponytail. He still loved watching her do that.

"I figured you are." She leaned down and straightened the welcome mat in front of the door, giving him a complete view of her cleavage. Was she doing this on purpose?

She straightened.

He blinked to shift his attention. "Well, I am. Very sorry."

"For what?"

"Everything—"

"No." She took a step closer to him. "What *specifically* are you sorry for?" She brushed past him to lean on the railing of the walkway. That wildflower scent trailed behind her. It'd only been two days since he'd seen her. The effect she had made it seem like years.

"Specifically? I...uh, I'm sorry about what I said."

She raised her eyebrows. Alright, she wanted something more specific than that. He'd give her anything she needed from him, as long as she'd come back. To him. He didn't care about the restaurant.

"I'm sorry I said you didn't understand anything about business. You do. I won't make excuses, but before I pushed you away, dozens of employees watched us. Trevor came up, excited the no-dating policy was gone. I panicked. All I could see were lawsuits, losing the business—"

"And since you're responsible for your brothers—"

She'd touched on that once before. But having to say it exposed his vulnerability. "Yes. That I'd let them down, too. And at that moment, I couldn't think of anything else but how to make sure I didn't ruin their future."

"Because you can't choose me over your brothers."

He winced. What kind of answer could he give her for that? He didn't have to choose. They were all equal.

She stepped closer.

He didn't move. The truth wasn't the quickest way to win her back, but she needed to hear it. "At the time, I didn't think I could choose you over them."

"I know, Brogan."

"You do?"

She nodded, her hair swinging softly with the motion. "Yes."

"I didn't realize I'd chosen them over you until I had about half a bottle of whiskey in me." He watched her a long moment, searching for a way to explain how different he'd become. "I'll never say I'm thankful for our fight. I hurt you, and I'm truly sorry for that."

"What do you want, Brogan?"

"I came to apologize."

Selena tilted her head to the side. "What do you want for the future? Not for your brothers. Not for me. Not for the restaurant. For you. What do *you* want?"

He didn't have to second guess himself. "You." He swallowed, nerves pegging him from all sides. "I wouldn't choose you over my brothers. I can't choose one person I love over the other. And I love you, Selena."

Surprise flickered in her eyes. "Did it take the whiskey for you to figure that out, too?"

"No." He reached out, skimming a finger lightly down the curve of her cheek. "I've suspected it for a while, now, but it took the whiskey to make me get out of my own way and acknowledge it."

"I love you, too, Brogan."

Relief rushed through his system. Hearing those words was step one.

"I'm not coming back to work at O'Keeley's."

"I didn't expect you, too. But I want to keep seeing you. Every day, if possible." He searched her face, trying to figure out the right way to ask. "I love you, Selena. And I want to marry you."

She took a sharp breath.

He rushed on before she could say yes or no. "It doesn't have to be this month or even this year, but I know you're who I want. If you'll have me."

She nodded and wrapped her arms around his neck, giving him a long hug. "Absolutely."

She kissed him lightly. Enough that it left him wanting more. When he began to wrap his arms tighter, she moved away.

"I love you, Brogan, and I do want to marry you." She had such a teasing expression he had to smile. The gorgeous, opinionated woman would be his wife someday. He'd do everything he could to make sure he kept her happy.

"But? You look like you were going to say something." He took a step. "Better yet, you can tell me later and let me kiss you until my brother's show up to help move?"

"No." She shook her head. "You can't. See, I do forgive

you for what you said. But, I still haven't exacted revenge for hiding me in the bathroom."

Wait. "But I thought the no-touching thing in the office was revenge."

"That was for hiding me under a desk."

He glanced down at her outfit, the skimpy thing that made him want to lock her in his bedroom for a full week. The sigh he heard escape his lips matched his mood at the realization of her payback. "You're going to make me suffer all day, aren't you?"

"That was the plan."

"You're mean."

"I guess you should know that before you marry me." She laughed, light and sexy.

"I love you," he murmured a second before he snatched her to his chest. "You'll have the next eighty years to exact your revenge on me."

EPILOGUE

Rian O'Keeley plated the sea bass and set the small garnish on the side. He picked up two plates and walked out of the kitchen at his childhood home and into the garden. Being back in Ireland at his old home, made the world feel a little smaller. The quietness. The smell of the damp earth. The chill in the air cooled his face after standing in front of his ma's old stove.

Brogan held Selena in his arms as he swayed gently to the sound of flutes filling the air. Cathal had decorated the garden, a thousand white lights surrounding the couple. His younger brother had always been dramatic.

"Here you go," Rian said as he set the two plates on the table.

Selena grinned. "Thank you! I'm starving." The ring on her finger caught Rian's eye. Brogan's proposal was epic. He'd brought Selena to Ireland and taken her on a long walk. At some point, he proposed since they returned with her wiping tears and wearing a small diamond ring that belonged to their ma.

Since neither he nor Cathal ever had any intention of getting married, they didn't object.

"I cannot believe that the three of you grew up in that small house." Selena sat down at the wrought iron table. "You're all so big."

Brogan patted Rian on the back as he passed by. "It was tight. I'm just happy to still have it in the family."

Rian wiped his hands on the towel slung over his shoulder. "I am, too. It will be a nice place to relax when I travel this way."

"I'd love to come here for our honeymoon." Selena took a sip of her wine. "If that's alright?"

Brogan sat back in disbelief. "Really? Here? I heard you mention before that you wanted to travel the world and see all the beautiful places. I figured we'd head over to Italy or France."

"You are marrying a woman of impeccable taste, Brog." Rian took a step back and held his hands out wide. "This is the most beautiful place on the planet." He turned and left the couple to their dinner.

After all the sacrifices Brogan made for the family, Rian could finally take a deep breath as the guilt released. Brogan had Selena.

The End

ABOUT THE AUTHOR

Palmer Jones writes fun and flirty, romantic fiction. Born and raised in the South, she loves to travel but will always call Georgia her home. With a degree in accounting, she spends part of her day immersed in numbers. The rest of the time is spent with her friends, family, and hiding away in the worlds she creates through her stories.

ACKNOWLEDGMENTS

I want to thank several people that helped with not only writing this book but also supporting me in so many ways. My husband, my parents, and my friends for listening to all my ramblings and reading my work.

Thank you to Jessie, for sticking with me throughout my crazy writing journey. Thank you Kim for being so supportive.

I'd also like to thank a few individuals who helped make this a great book. JD&J Design for the beautiful cover. Patricia Ogilvie for helping put the final touches on the book.

Made in the USA
Middletown, DE
15 September 2020